TILL THE SUN GROWS COLD

John W. Bebout

I love thee, I love but thee
  With a love that shall not die
  Till the sun grows cold
  And the stars grow old.

--BAYARD TAYLOR

This book is dedicated, with love, to my children: Jonathan, Patrick, Andrew, Nicole McGoodwin and Lauren Kipling

CHAPTER 1

No man chooses evil because it is evil; he only mistakes it for happiness, the good he seeks. —Mary Wollstonecraft

Two men walked their horses single file down the dirt road. It was late May, and the air was hot and heavy with moisture. There was no breeze and dust swirled around the horses' hooves, hanging in the still air long after the riders had passed. The man in front had perfectly trimmed white whiskers and wore a straw planter's hat; the second man looked like a farm hand, with a soft felt hat and a scruffy beard. But despite their civilian clothes, even the most casual observer would notice the unmistakable military bearing of the riders: they rode with perfect posture, their heels down and their backs ramrod straight.

The man with the white whiskers turned to the other man. "How far are we from Fort Donelson, lieutenant?"

"I reckon about seven or 8 miles, colonel, rounds 'bout halfway to Fort Henry."

The colonel nodded and continued to study the sides of the road as he passed by. After traveling a few hundred yards more, he stopped his horse and dismounted. He handed his reins to the lieutenant and walked to the south side of the road where a small stream had cut a steep embankment. After examining both banks of the stream, he turned and walked to the north side of the road. He nodded his head in satisfaction as he noted that the land rose slowly to a small ridgeline, perhaps 15 feet above the elevation of the roadway. *This will do just fine*, he thought.

The colonel walked over to some shade beneath a large oak tree and motioned to the lieutenant to join him. He removed his straw hat and wiped his brow with a red bandana. "Blaze this tree, lieutenant, as I want no mistakes or misunderstandings. I have seen no better place than this to launch our attack."

After the lieutenant had removed a piece of bark with his knife, leaving a clearly visible scar, the colonel led the lieutenant to the bank of the stream. Pointing, the colonel said, "I want gun pits dug on the other side of the stream, mebbe twenty-five yards south. But make sure they have a clear view of the opposite embankment." Turning back, they walked to the north side of the road and the colonel pointed up the hillside. "And put gun pits up there at the top of the ridgeline. Again, make sure you have clear line-of-sight to the roadway."

As they walked back to the shade, the colonel began to explain his plan. The lieutenant wiped his eyes with his sleeve and studied the man as he spoke. They had served together almost since the beginning of the War, and he recognized the muted excitement in the colonel's voice as he planned the fight. The lieutenant had seen it many times before. As usual, the colonel left as little as possible to chance. The colonel ended his explanation with, "We can prevail only with complete surprise."

The lieutenant did not share the colonel's excitement. Four years of killing had been enough for him; he knew that the War had tainted his humanity and stained his soul. He just wanted to try and forget what he had seen and done. When the lieutenant nodded his understanding, the colonel seemed to sense his reticence and placed his hand on the lieutenant's shoulder. "One more fight, Frank," the colonel said. "Just one more fight."

Around 7:00 a.m. three days later, Major Gordon French left Fort Donelson to make the roughly seventeen mile overland trip to Fort Henry. French was the Union paymaster and he had been entrusted with nearly $30,000 in gold and silver coins to pay the soldiers being mustered out of the Army at the fort.

The major was a cautious man and had put together a substantial convoy. There were eleven military escorts traveling on foot, and one covered wagon carrying a heavy, tarp-covered lock box. The non-commissioned officer leading the soldiers—'non-com,' for short—was armed with a revolver while the men carried a mixture of single-shot muskets and carbines. Major French, who rode in the wagon with the civilian driver, was unarmed.

The convoy made no better than two miles per hour and finally reached the vicinity of the blazed tree around 11:00 a.m. The mood was light because the War had finally been declared officially over only five days earlier, and the major joked and chatted with the civilian driver the entire trip. He was in a fine mood, and he was looking forward to returning to his home and family. "Enough of military life for me," he told the driver. "I intend to..." But no one will ever know what the major intended to do. A single gunshot rang out and one of the mules fell dead in its traces, disabling the wagon. That was immediately followed by a barrage of gunfire from somewhere up on the hillside and the Major was killed where he sat. The driver was wounded, but he managed to dive for cover under the wagon.

Sergeant Christian Fenter, the non-com in charge of the escort, threw himself to the ground at the sound of the first gunshot. The gunshots seemed to be coming from a low ridge on the north side of the road, but he could not be certain. Every time he raised his head to look, minié balls and Spencer rounds fell around him, kicking up angry spouts of dust. His men, none of whom had been in combat before, stood in the open roadway firing blindly up the hillside. He watched as three of them fell wounded or dead in the road within seconds. "Down!" he yelled. "Get down!"

Sergeant Fenter looked around desperately for cover. Behind

him he saw the small stream and its embankment. He grabbed the leg of one soldier that was rushing past him and ordered, "Fall back to the stream bed!"

Sergeant Fenter crawled on his stomach towards a group of four soldiers taking cover behind the wagon with the civilian driver. When he reached them, he sat with his back against the wagon wheel. Splinters of wood rained down on him and the men as bullets tore through the wooden wagon. When he had caught his breath, he said, "When I say 'go,' run for that stream behind us as fast as you can. There is protection there. I will cover you as best I am able."

Sergeant Fenter checked his revolver, then yelled 'go!' At the same instant, he stood up and began firing up the hill as fast as he could cock and pull the trigger. He watched as the first man made it to the stream bed, but the second was shot before he had taken three steps. The remaining men leapt over the soldier's body and threw themselves behind the embankment.

Sergeant Fenter ducked back down behind the wagon. It seemed all the enemy's fire was now directed at him. Bullets ricocheted off the packed earth and buzzed angrily around him. He knew that if he stayed there, the shooters would ultimately flank him and kill him.

Sergeant Fenter holstered his revolver and took a deep breath. Then he screamed at the top of his lungs and ran for the stream. He was immediately struck in the leg, but his momentum carried him to the embankment. His soldiers pulled him over the edge and under cover.

The sergeant cried out through clenched teeth and fought to keep himself conscious. The pain from his leg wound was all consuming and he found it difficult to think clearly. He glanced around and made a quick count: seven men, including he and the civilian driver, had made it to the ravine. Of these, three men, besides himself, were wounded. They all sat with their backs to the ravine wall as bullets buzzed over their heads.

Sergeant Fenter dragged himself in front of the men. Their eyes were wide with fear. He addressed them with a calmness he did not feel: "We can make a stand here, boys. Now, I want you to reload your weapons if you have not already done so. Then we will spread out along the stream. Prepare to return fire on my command. Understand?"

The men nodded. "Yes, sergeant," they answered.

The colonel watched from his hidden gun pit behind the embankment as the wounded sergeant began to spread his men out along the little stream. The colonel whispered to his men, "Wait until I fire, then fire at will." The colonel raised his musket, sighted on Sergeant Fenter's back and squeezed the trigger.

CHAPTER 2

The Letter

Fort Donelson, Tennessee

To Mr. Merritt Cowles, Sr.
Columbus, Ohio
Dear Mr. Cowles,

It is with regret that I announce to you that your son was killed on May 31, 1865, while executing his duties as a military escort for a payroll wagon train. All indications are that he did not linger with his wounds and perished with little pain.

He was universally beloved in the Regiment, but more particularly in our Company where he was better known. By his death, the Regiment loses the services of one whose place it will be difficult to fill. In passing this tribute to his memory I but re-echo the sentiments of the entire command. I sincerely sympathize with you in the irreparable loss you have sustained, whereby you have lost a kind and faithful son. May his soul rest in peace.

Our lieutenant, whose name is Thomas Jacobs will be in your city to speak to the Chamber of Commerce on June 24-25. I think you will find him at the Neil House or somewhere in that vicinity. He can give you more information about your son's death than I possibly can give you on paper.

Wishing your sorrows may be alleviated by the consolation of knowing that he died a glorious death in service to his Country.
I remain,
Your Obedient Servant,
Sergt. Hubert Parnell, Co. B,

71st OVI

Merritt Allen Cowles, Sr., read the letter repeatedly, until he had memorized every line and every punctuation mark. Then he read it again. It was in this way that he hoped to numb himself to the horrible reality of it all. But nothing could alleviate the terrible darkness and sense of loss that had overtaken his soul.

Merritt remained in his chair, unmoving, as the day turned to night. He neither ate nor drank. Finally, he rose from his chair and lit an oil lamp. He poured a brandy and stood staring at himself in a mirror over the fireplace mantle. Even to his own eyes, he appeared beaten down, *chewed up and spit out*, as they say. He was shrunken and pale and dark circles had appeared under his eyes. He ran his hands through his greying hair and fought the urge to drop to his knees and scream his son's name.

There were two daguerreotypes on the mantle. One was of his wife Sadie who had died 3 years earlier. She was wearing a black dress with a white lace collar, her dark hair pulled tightly back and parted in the center, with the hint of a smile at the corners of her mouth. Her cheeks had been tinted a healthy pink by the photographer. She was holding Merritt Allen Cowles, Jr., whom they called 'Allen,' and who looked to be about 2-years-old. The second photograph was of Allen in his new army uniform, sitting stiffly in front of an American flag, holding a Colt Army revolver across his chest.

Merritt Sr. reached out and gently touched the frame of his wife's photograph. He whispered, "Oh, Sadie, my only comfort is the knowledge that you now hold our boy safely to your bosom." He then turned to his son's photograph. He gave a deep sigh and was about to say something when he felt a crushing pain in his chest. He could neither breathe nor call out and he collapsed to the floor. His vision blurred and then all became darkness.

Night had become day again when Merritt awoke, sweat-soaked and disoriented. For one brief, blissful moment, he had no memory of his losses. But then they came flooding back, washing over him in waves of despair and pain. He struggled up from the floor and tried to walk out of the room, but he made it no farther than a nearby chair. His left arm ached, and he felt nauseous. He thought he might be dying, but he felt no fear. *Is it a sin to want to die?* he wondered. He collapsed into the chair and closed his eyes.

When Merritt again awoke, the sun was high in the sky. He stood up carefully and walked to the kitchen where he filled a basin with water. The nausea had passed although his arm continued to ache. He washed his face and forced himself to eat some fruit from a bowl on the table left by his housekeeper. It had no flavor to him, but he knew that he needed some nourishment to abate his waning strength.

Merritt attempted to calm his mind. He tried to remember what day of the month it was, but he could not. He searched through a pile of unopened mail and found the most recent edition of The Daily Ohio Statesman newspaper. It said 'June 24, 1865.'

Merritt threw the newspaper on a table. He determined to go find Lieutenant Thomas Jacobs before he left the city.

Merritt rode his horse to the corner of State and High Street where the Clinton Bank stood. It was a three-story brick building attached on one side to a haberdashery. It was much like the other buildings on the street and only the two ornate columns around the front door gave a hint of the building's purpose.

Merritt walked through the lobby towards the offices in the back, collecting condolences from various employees along the way. He stopped at a doorway labeled 'Andrew Jackson Brazile,

Vice President,' straightened his tie, and knocked. Without waiting for a reply, he walked into the office.

Andrew Jackson Brazile, 'Jackie', as he liked to be called, jumped to his feet. "Mr. Cowles!" he exclaimed. "We did not expect you to come in today. Your housekeeper sent word of your son. We were all so sorry to hear of your loss..."

Merritt sat down in a chair facing Jackie's desk. "Thank you, Jackie."

"Can I get you anything?"

"No, no. This will only take a moment. But I do have something important to tell you."

Jackie clasped his hands on his desk and looked expectantly at Merritt. Merritt said, "I am stepping down as President of this bank, Jackie, and I would like you to take over."

Jackie's mouth fell open. "I... I do not know what to say."

Merritt smiled at Jackie. He was a good man and a hard worker. He had been employed at the bank since Merritt's father had founded it more than twenty years earlier. "Say 'yes,' Jackie. You have earned it and I no longer have the heart for it."

After leaving the bank, Merritt rode slowly down State Street towards the *Neil House*, which was a five-story brick hotel across the street from the Ohio State House. He knew the way well, having attended numerous political functions there over the years. The *Neil House* was one of the finest hotels in Columbus and was frequented by state politicians and well-heeled travelers alike.

Merritt gave his horse to the valet and checked his pocket watch as he walked into the hotel. Not yet 5:00 o'clock. Too early for the Chamber of Commerce meeting, he thought, but maybe the lieutenant is staying at the hotel. He passed a poster in the lobby as he was making his way to the registration desk to ask for Lieutenant Jacobs. It had a line drawing of a handsome young man in a Union uniform with lieutenant's bars on his epaulettes. The poster read: 'Lieutenant Thomas Jacobs will speak tonight on the glorious exploits of the 71st Ohio Volunteer Infantry Regiment during the late Rebellion. 8:00 p.m. in the Washington Room. All welcome!'

Merritt was walking past the open door to the bar when he noticed a man in uniform sitting alone at a table. He immediately recognized him from the poster. Merritt walked up to him and asked, "Lieutenant Jacobs?"

The man looked up at Merritt and said, "I am."

"I am Merritt Cowles..."

"You are Allen's Daddy?" the lieutenant interrupted. He jumped to his feet and extended his hand. "I am so sorry for your loss, Sir, Allen was a fine boy and a good soldier."

"Thank you, lieutenant. That means a great deal to me."

The lieutenant indicated for Merritt to sit down. "Can I get you a drink?" he asked.

Merritt shook his head. "No thank you. But I would appreciate whatever information you can give me about Allen's death. Sergeant Parnell's letter to me seemed to hint that there was more to the story."

"Ah," said the lieutenant, "then it is I who will need another drink." He caught the bartender's eye and pointed to his empty glass. In a moment, his glass was refilled. The lieutenant took a sip and asked Merritt, "How much do you know?"

Merritt thought that was an odd question. "How much? Only what was in the sergeant's letter: that Allen was killed while guarding a paymaster's wagon train."

The lieutenant placed his drink on the table. "A tragic event and an embarrassment to the Army," he said. He lowered his voice and glanced quickly around. "There is an ongoing investigation. I am not supposed to discuss it with anyone. But the Army is not good at investigating itself and I fear that nothing will ever come of the inquiry." The lieutenant picked up his drink, drained it and looked around again for the bartender. He asked Merritt, "Were you ever in the Military?"

"I fought in Mexico."

The lieutenant nodded. "Then you know how it works. The

brass protects itself. Always has, always will."

"Are you saying that someone in the military had something to do with my son's death?"

The lieutenant glanced around quickly again. "I ain't sayin' that. I am just saying that something about this whole thing stinks." The lieutenant started to signal for the bartender again when Merritt held his arm. "Let us go to the restaurant and we can talk over dinner."

CHAPTER 3

The Details Emerge

It is the absence of facts that frightens people: the gap you open, into which they pour their fears, fantasies, desires.
—Hilary Mantel

The restaurant at the Neil House was one of the most popular in Columbus. Even early in the evening, nearly every table was filled with prosperous looking men sipping whiskey from crystal tumblers. Waiters with white aprons bustled about, weaving between the tables, carrying teetering trays of food and drink.

Merritt led the lieutenant across the restaurant to a table in the back. Merritt was well-known to nearly all the patrons and they rose from their seats as he passed by to express their condolences for the loss of his son. Merritt thanked each of them but did not linger to talk. He was anxious to hear what the lieutenant had to say.

Merritt ordered steak for the lieutenant and nothing for himself. Merritt had no appetite. "I have no desire to compromise you in any way, lieutenant, but I would be grateful if you shared the details of my son's death with me."

Lieutenant Jacobs placed his knife and fork on the plate and pushed it to the side. He gave a sigh and said, "I owe that much to

Allen. He was a fine soldier."

"Were you with him when he died?" Merritt asked.

The lieutenant shook his head. "No. When the paymaster did not show up at Fort Henry on time, I was sent out with a small patrol to look for him."

"Sergeant Parnell gave me no details other than Allen was guarding a payroll wagon train. So, this was a robbery?"

The lieutenant nodded. "They took around $30,000 in gold and silver coins."

Merritt's eyes widened. "So much? I cannot imagine that there are more than one hundred men stationed at Fort Henry."

"Normally so. But with the War over, both Fort Henry and Fort Donelson are being used to muster out returning soldiers."

"Tell me about the convoy."

The lieutenant sat back in his chair. "It was sizeable," he said. "There were eleven military escorts, including your son and one non-commissioned officer named Fenter. The men travelled on foot. The payroll was carried in a single lock box in a covered wagon driven by a civilian employee. The paymaster, Major French, he rode on the wagon."

Merritt took a sip of water and shook his head. "That is a lot of firepower. How many men attacked them?"

"We do not know for sure, but from footprints and other evidence, we suspect no more than six or 7 men."

Merritt was shocked that so few men could overpower twelve armed soldiers, but before he could say anything, the lieutenant added, "It was an ambush, both clever and deadly."

"Have the survivors been able to tell you anything about the attackers?"

Lieutenant Jacobs dropped his eyes. "There were no survivors."

"None?" Merritt asked incredulously. When the lieutenant said no more, Merritt pressed him. "There is more to this story than you are telling me."

Lieutenant Jacobs would not meet Merritt's eyes. "There is some evidence that those men not killed outright in the ambush were executed."

Merritt dropped his water glass, making a clatter so loud that the entire restaurant looked up and a busboy came running. Merritt felt the now-familiar tightening in his chest and the room began to spin. He thanked the lieutenant profusely and quickly made his way out of the restaurant and into the fresh evening air. There he leaned unsteadily against a wall, gasped for breath, and willed the attack to subside.

Merritt awoke unrefreshed after a restless night. He had dreamed of his son's detachment fighting for their lives. The dream had been so realistic that he could smell the fear and burnt gunpowder in the air; but when the fighting had stopped and all had become quiet, a deep sense of dread had enveloped him. Even in his dream, he had tried to cover his ears so as not to hear the methodical 'bang,' pause, 'bang,' pause, 'bang' of the *coups de grâce* that followed. "No!" he had screamed, the sound of it echoing endlessly around his bedroom, startling him awake.

Merritt forced himself to eat breakfast. The two attacks that had happened him had given him an increased sense of urgency to find his son's killers, and he wrestled with what to do next. More time was never a guarantee in this world, and he wanted... what? Revenge? Justice? *I do not really care how it is characterized,* he thought. *I just want them dead.*

While his housekeeper bustled about, a plan began to form in his mind. He asked the housekeeper if she would fetch the boy next door to send a telegram for him. "And tell him there is a dime in it for his trouble," Merritt added.

While the housekeeper was gone, Merritt began to write:

From: Merritt Cowles, Sr., Columbus, Ohio, 25 June
To: Honorable Allan Pinkerton, Pinkerton Detective Agency, Chicago, Illinois

Subject: I request the services of one of your best detectives
              for an indeterminate period not to exceed one (1)

year to investigate an Army payroll robbery that occurred near Fort Donelson, Tenn. on May 31, 1865. I will bear all costs including expenses. If agreeable, have the detective meet me in Nashville, Tennessee at the St. Cloud Hotel on July 18. Please advise at once.

In less than 2 hours, Merritt had his reply:

The American Telegraph Co.

From   ALLAN PINKERTON. CHICAGO ILL. JUNE XXV.
To   MERRITT COWLES SR. COLUMBUS OHIO

I HAVE ASSIGNED DETECTIVE KATE WARNE TO ASSIST YOU. SHE WILL MEET YOU IN NASHVILLE AT THE PLACE AND TIME YOU REQUESTED. YOUR SERVANT, ALLAN PINKERTON.

Merritt folded the telegram and put it in his pocket. *A female detective?* He knew that there had been several successful female spies during the War. Well, he was willing to reserve judgement. It was a different world than it had been before the War.

Merritt was sitting in the lobby of the St. Cloud Hotel in Nashville when a Bellboy tapped him on the shoulder. "For you, Sir," the boy said, handing Merritt a folded piece of blue paper. It said simply, 'I am in the Lobby Bar -Kate Warne.'

Merritt rose from his chair and walked to the entrance of the bar that occupied one corner of the lobby. Inside he saw mostly men, but one woman sat alone at a table in the back. She was wearing a brown skirt and a twill jacket closed at the neck with a cameo. On the chair next to her lay a brown fedora.

Merritt stopped short as he approached her. He had not expected the detective to be such a beautiful woman. He felt as awkward as a schoolboy and willed himself not to stumble as he approached her table. He noticed the faint scent of jasmine as he stood before her.

Kate rose to her feet. "Mr. Cowles?"

Merritt extended his hand. "I am. And you are Miss Warne?"

"Mrs. Warne," Kate said. She shook Merritt's hand and showed him a small wallet with a brass badge and an ID card declaring her a 'Special Detective' with the Pinkerton National Detective Agency, Incorporated. She asked Merritt to sit down.

Merritt thought Mrs. Warne even more attractive up close. She had dark hair with soft curls that framed her face, and her eyes were a remarkable shade of green. She asked, "May I get you a drink, Mr. Cowles?"

"In a moment, perhaps." Merritt sat down and tried not to stare at Kate. "Mr. Pinkerton promised me his best detective. Are you she?"

A slight smile pulled at the corners of Kate's mouth. "I cannot imagine Mr. Pinkerton promising his worst detective."

"Nonetheless..."

Kate held up her hands. "Nonetheless, you have every right to know what kind of a pig you got from Mr. Pinkerton's poke."

Merritt smiled. "Just so," he said.

Kate gave Merritt a quick synopsis of her life with nei-ther braggadocio nor false modesty: newly widowed, she had sought employment with the Pinkerton Detective Agency. At the Agency, she had helped save Lincoln from an assassination plot in Baltimore and had been personally responsible for recovering tens of thousands of dollars in stolen money and the capture of several well-known bank robbers.

Merritt was duly impressed. When Kate had finished her story, Merritt said, "Thank you, Mrs. Warne. I believe we will work well together."

Kate nodded her head and said, "What can you tell me about the payroll robbery? Mr. Pinkerton had few details."

Merritt pulled the letter he had received about Allen's death from his coat pocket and handed it to Kate. She studied the letter for a few moments and then handed it back to Merritt. "I am sorry for your loss, Mr. Cowles."

"There is more to the story," Merritt said. "I met with an Army lieutenant named Jacobs who had been sent to look for the payroll wagon train when it did not arrive at Fort Henry. He provided me with two details not mentioned in Sergeant Parnell's letter. One, he believes that someone high-up in the military is responsible for the robbery and, two, all survivors from the ambush had been executed."

Kate grew pale. "And my role?"

"I expect you to help me find the killers."

"And then?"

"And then?" repeated Merritt. *And then I will kill them all*, he thought. But he said instead, "and then we will turn them in to the authorities."

Kate nodded. "Good," she said. "Know that I will have no part in a vendetta."

CHAPTER 4

The Scene of the Crime

Nightly you retrace your steps again to return to the scene of the crime. It's uncanny how you hover in the air of the wreckage that you left behind. —Aimee Mann

Merritt spent the next day outfitting Kate and himself for the eighty-five mile trip from Nashville to Fort Donelson. He rented two horses and bought a brand new carbine for himself. Kate provided her own weapons: a Colt revolver she carried in a holster worn outside her jacket and an evil-looking, short-barreled shotgun.

Once they reached Fort Donelson, they followed the north route to Fort Henry, the same one Lieutenant Jacobs said the paymaster had taken. They passed through lush farmland and deep woods. It was peaceful, almost idyllic, but Merritt took no pleasure from it. He saw it only as the setting for his son's death, a cruel denouement to a tragic play. A darkness settled over him, giving him chills even in the summer heat.

"We are here," announced Kate as she stopped her horse. Merritt trotted up beside her and looked around. It seemed no different to him than any other spot they had passed along the way. "How do you know?"

Kate pointed to a tree with a fresh blaze on it. "Did Lieutenant

Jacobs say that he had marked the spot of the ambush?" Kate asked.

"Not that I recall."

Kate dismounted and walked her horse over to some shade. After tying the horse to a small tree, she walked to the North side of the road and stood looking up the small hill. She pointed to a pile of dead brush at the top of the hill and asked Merritt, "See that? There is no natural reason for so much dead wood to be there. That brush has been cut."

Merritt tied his horse and joined Kate as she climbed the hill. At the top, they saw that shallow pits had been dug behind the brush piles. Kate stepped into one and looked carefully at the ground. Rainstorms since the ambush had erased any footprints, but she found several brass cartridges. She showed one to Merritt: ".50 caliber, rim fire. There was at least one carbine up here."

Merritt looked through the dead brush at the road below. *Sitting ducks*, he thought. He would not let his mind dwell on the terror that his son must have felt when the ambush began. Merritt said, "Lieutenant Jacobs told me that there were six or 7 men involved in the ambush. Clearly, not all were up here. There is simply not enough room."

Kate nodded in agreement as she placed the brass cartridges in her pocket. She and Merritt searched several hundred yards on either side of the gun pits but found nothing. "The rest of them had to be across the road somewhere on the other side of the stream," Kate concluded.

Merritt and Kate climbed down the hill and approached the stream which had eroded the road-side bank to around three or 4 feet. Kate crouched down to examine the embankment and said, "The convoy must have thought this good cover."

Merritt shivered as a chill moved down his spine. "To their peril," he said glumly, "Lieutenant Jacobs told me that he found seven of the thirteen men in the convoy dead against that bank."

Kate nodded and said, "It was a deadly trap." She turned to cross the stream when Merritt suddenly leaned heavily against her, almost sagging to the ground. Kate helped Merritt stagger to some shade where she gave him water from a canteen. "Are you alright?" she asked.

"This place," Merritt said, barely above a whisper. "I thought I could bear it here, but I cannot. I see everything through my poor Allen's eyes, I hear everything through his ears. There are ghosts here and they call out to me."

Kate placed her hand on Merritt's shoulder. She felt Merritt trembling and her concern grew as she watched him grow pale. "Mr. Cowles," Kate said. When Merritt did not respond, she said more loudly, "Mr. Cowles, listen to me."

Merritt raised his eyes to Kate's, and she said, "I, too, hear the ghosts here. They cry out for justice. And you and I will give it to them, Mr. Cowles. Do you understand?"

Merritt nodded, suddenly embarrassed by his own fragility. He felt deeply humiliated and dropped his eyes from Kate's. Kate got up and handed the canteen to Merritt. "Now, you wait here while I finish my survey and then we can leave this evil place."

Kate thought about Merritt as she crossed the little stream. She sensed that the fear and vulnerability that had washed over Merritt only a few moments before were new emotions to him. But Kate had seen it many times before during the War: men being crushed by grief and beaten into despair and ineffectiveness. Many of these men had been bigger than life and charged through life, yet all were suddenly diminished by their own helplessness at the loss of a comrade or family member. In Kate's experience, this led to one of two outcomes: for some, grief morphed into a fury that filled their bellies with anger, both raging hot and righteous. But others remained meek and paralyzed and were unable to take decisive action. *Which one*, she wondered, *would Merritt be*?

Merritt watched as Kate crossed the creek looking for the ambush site on the other side. He got to his feet and walked unsteadily to the bank of the stream where he washed his face with the cool water. When he was finished, he turned his face towards heaven and softly recited a verse from Romans. As a child,

Merritt's minister had used it as a warning to the boys for bad behavior in Sunday school. But now, it took on a new and terrible meaning: *For the one in authority is God's servant for your good. But if you do wrong, be afraid, for rulers do not bear the sword for no reason. They are God's servants, agents of wrath to bring punishment on the wrongdoer.*

While Merritt sat in the shade sipping water from a canteen, Kate returned from the woods behind the stream. She came back carrying another brass cartridge. "How are you feeling?" she asked Merritt.

"Better." He handed the canteen to Kate who sat down heavily in the shade beside him. After several long swallows, Kate said, "I believe Lieutenant Jacobs is correct; it would appear there must be a military man involved." Merritt raised his eyebrows as Kate continued: "This ambush was undertaken with military precision. How else could six or 7 men defeat a force of nearly twice as many men?"

Kate took another swallow of water and handed the canteen back to Merritt. "There are gun pits about twenty yards on the other side of the stream. They have a perfect view of the opposite bank where the men's bodies were found. I suspect the men atop the hill started the attack, driving the escort to cover along the stream. When the time was right, the men hidden in the gun pits on the other side of the stream opened fire, catching them in a cross-fire."

"But why kill them all?"

Kate shrugged. "I would guess it was to insure there were no witnesses. Which again suggests a military connection; at least some of the attackers were probably known to the military escort."

"Then that gives us a place to start," said Merritt.

CHAPTER 5

Dover, Tennessee

Not knowing how near the truth is, we seek it far away.
—Hakuin

Merritt and Kate made their way back to Fort Donelson. The sun was high in a cloudless sky and there was little sound beyond the buzzing of the horse flies that tortured the horses and riders alike as they walked. But, somehow, the sun seemed a little brighter and the sky a little bluer the farther they got from the site of the ambush.

There was little conversation as they rode, each one lost in their own thoughts. The trip back passed quickly and soon the earthworks and abattis that surrounded Fort Donelson loomed into view. They were part of a more than 3-mile arc which enclosed a bluff north of the fort and the town of Dover to the south. To Merritt, the defenses looked very daunting, and he wondered at the bravery of the men who had attacked them.

U. S. Grant had captured Fort Donelson in 1862 and the Confederates had tried on two subsequent occasions to recapture it, once in mid-1862 and again in the winter of 1863. Both attempts had failed, but evidence of the sieges and battles was everywhere. The town of Dover had lost every building save four in the second Confederate attack. But now, just 2-years later, the wounds of war were slowly beginning to heal; Merritt saw wild-flowers growing on the earthworks and cattle grazing among the abattis.

Merritt and Kate crossed the earthworks a few hundred yards west of Dover. As they made their way into town, they passed clusters of small log cabins which had been used to house the Fort's soldiers. Each cabin had a fireplace, straw on a dirt floor and a canvas roof. Merritt wondered if Allen had been bivou-acked in one of them. They appeared tiny and a bit forlorn and many were in disrepair. Torn sheets of canvas from the roofs flapped in the wind, startling the horses.

Although no one would call Dover a thriving community, most of the wrecked buildings had been cleared and there was a fair amount of reconstruction. Merritt reckoned that perhaps two-hundred people lived there. He and Kate made their way across town to the *Dover Hotel* where Merritt had learned that Colonel William W. Lowe had his headquarters.

The *Dover Hotel* was a two-story clapboard structure that sat adjacent to the Cumberland River. Porches on the first and sec-ond stories faced the street and ran the length of the building. Merritt and Kate entered the building without being challenged. In the parlor, they found a junior officer reading a newspaper. He neither looked up nor stood up when they approached.

"We would like to see Colonel Lowe," Merritt said.

"He is busy," the officer answered.

"Then we will wait."

The officer frowned and folded his newspaper. "Do you have an appointment?" he asked.

"No. But we would like to talk to him regarding an important matter."

The officer stood up. "Your names?"

Before Merritt could answer, Kate said, "Mr. and Mrs. Merritt."

The officer nodded and walked over to a closed door at the back of the parlor. He knocked and entered. A moment later, he opened the door and motioned to Merritt and Kate to enter. As he left the room, he closed the door behind him.

Colonel Lowe sat behind a large banker's desk which was covered with towering piles of papers. He had dark, thinning hair and a full, curly beard. His piercing blue eyes looked out at the world over a long, aquiline nose. When Kate walked into the room, he jumped to his feet. "Madam!" he said, reaching for her hand. "My adjutant tells me that you seek my assistance." Kate smiled and said, "Mr. Cowles and I would be most grateful, colonel."

"Cowles?" asked the colonel. "I was told your name was Merritt..."

Kate gave Colonel Lowe one of her dazzling smiles. "I am so sorry, colonel," she said, "we wished to keep a degree of anonymity."

Colonel Lowe smiled back and reluctantly dropped Kate's hand to shake Merritt's. "My, but this all seems mysterious," he said as he sat down. "What may I do for you?"

Merritt glanced at the piles of papers on the colonel's desk and said, "We will try and be brief, colonel."

Colonel Lowe smiled and waved dismissively at the papers. "These papers represent the minutiae associated with running a military facility in peacetime. There is little good to say about war, except that it de-empathizes the trivial." He added, "I welcome a brief distraction."

Merritt got right to the point: "We would like to talk to you about your payroll robbery last May."

The smile vanished from Colonel Lowe's face. "May I ask how this is of concern to you?"

"My son Allen was one of the military guards killed during the robbery."

Colonel Lowe's eyes widened. "Allen Cowles, of course! I should have recognized your name. You have my deepest sympathy, Mr. Cowles."

"Thank you, colonel. Mrs. Warne is a Pinkerton Detective assisting me and we have some questions about the robbery."

Colonel Lowe sat back in his chair and studied Kate. He suddenly remembered why he knew her name. "Ah, Mrs. Warne," he said, "I have read about you. You are the woman who saved Lincoln's life in Baltimore."

Kate nodded slightly. "Detective," she said.

"Detective?"

"The 'Detective' who saved Lincoln's life," she said. "I find an accounting of my sex superfluous."

The colonel blushed. His mouth worked but no sound came out. Merritt rushed to the colonel's rescue: "The Country certainly owes Mrs. Warne a debt of gratitude, colonel, as I am certain you would agree. But to the matter at hand..."

Colonel Lowe looked down at his hands and then back at Merritt. "I am sorry but there is little I am permitted to say. The Army has formed a commission to investigate the robbery..."

"Yes, I know, we have been so informed," interrupted Merritt. "We were also told that you suspect someone in the military was involved."

Colonel Lowe's eyes widened. "That is a sensitive matter, Mr. Cowles, perhaps best left to the military. And as I have said, I have no authorization to discuss this matter with civilians."

Kate spoke up, "I can assure you, colonel, that I operate with the full support and authority of the Pinkerton Detective Agency." Although he would not admit it to Merritt or Kate, Colonel Lowe was greatly displeased by the glacial pace at which the Army's investigation was moving. *Perhaps, Pinkerton involvement might speed things along,* he thought. "I must have your word that you will not conflict with, nor hinder, the Army's investigation," he said.

"Of course."

"And tell me who told you that we suspect some military involvement in the robbery."

Merritt shook his head. "That I cannot do. It was just a rumor we picked up," he lied. He did not want to implicate Lieutenant Jacobs.

Colonel Lowe did not believe Merritt's explanation, but he said, "Alright, tell me what you know and what you suspect, and I will try to fill in any blanks."

Merritt and Kate told the colonel about their visit to the ambush site and what they had learned and what they had inferred. Colonel Lowe would occasionally interrupt with questions or nod and say, 'That is much as it was told to me.'

After they had finished, Colonel Lowe offered them a drink. When they declined, the colonel poured himself a shot of whiskey and sat back in his chair. "I cannot deny that there was a military precision to the ambush. But I am not sure knowing that helps much. After all, the country is awash in ex-military men."

Kate nodded in agreement. "But what about the paymaster's route and schedule? That had to be a carefully kept secret."

"It was. Major French, the paymaster, took his job very seriously. I doubt that he told more than one or 2 other people in advance."

"Do you know who he might have told?" Merritt asked.

Colonel Lowe sensed that he had already said too much. He drained his whiskey and placed his glass on his desk. "I am afraid I have told you all I can." It was apparent to Merritt and Kate that the interview was over. "Well, Mrs. Warne, Mr. Cowles," said the colonel, "the stack of papers on my desk grows no shorter."

Merritt and Kate stood up and thanked Colonel Lowe for his time. As they left the office, they saw the young officer once again sitting on the sofa reading the newspaper. He did not look up and he said nothing as they passed by.

Merritt and Kate found lodging in a boarding house in Dover near the river. The boarding house was a private residence where the owner rented out two small bedrooms and provided breakfast and dinner. The house showed some signs of battle damage and bullet holes could be seen in the external planking.

After dinner, Merritt and Kate sat in two rockers on the front porch. Merritt lit a pipe and blew smoke at the evening sky. "What did you think of Colonel Lowe?" he asked Kate.

"I think the good colonel began to have second thoughts about sharing information from the investigation with us."

Merritt nodded in agreement. "Ultimately, I do not feel we learned much new."

"Maybe. But if the colonel is to be believed—and I see no reason why he should not—very few people knew of the schedule ahead of time. That is valuable as it limits the number of potential informants."

"I agree." Merritt tapped the ashes from his pipe and stood up. "I was hoping you could pull some strings. If we could get a list of these suspects from the Army, it would save us a great deal of time. And I do not believe the Army would refuse to share the preliminary results of their investigation with the Pinkertons."

"I had the same thought," said Kate. "In the morning, I will send a telegraph to Mr. Pinkerton."

CHAPTER 6

Dreams and Memories

I know that's what people say-- you'll get over it. I'd say it, too. But I know it's not true. Oh, you'll be happy again, never fear. But you won't forget. Every time you fall in love it will be because something in the man reminds you of him. —Betty Smith, A Tree Grows in Brooklyn

Kate had not expected sleep to come easily, and it did not. After tossing and turning for several hours, she wrapped herself in a blanket and stepped out onto the balcony. Somewhere nearby, a dove was singing her mournful song and peepers called to one another from the treetops. The air was still and cool and a million stars twinkled in the sky.

Kate was leaning against the railing when she saw the flash of a match along the shore of the river. In the flare of light, she recognized Merritt lighting his pipe. Apparently, he could not sleep either. Kate was not yet sure what she thought about Merritt. Except for his breakdown at the ambush site, he had kept his emotions carefully in check. But his company was easy to take, and he was a handsome man, taller than average with salt-and-pepper hair and warm brown eyes. And she had caught him looking at her when he thought she did not notice.

Kate laughed. *How old are you? She asked herself. Sixteen?* She turned and went back to bed. She lay in the dark and thought about the only two men she had ever loved: Her late husband Jimmy and a Pinkerton Detective named Timothy Webster.

Kate could never think about Jimmy without smiling. She was 22 years old when she met him, old enough to be considered a spinster by the standards of the time. Not that she had not been pursued by men; but Kate had simply never met a man before Jimmy with whom she desired to spend her life.

When she thought about it, Kate suspected that Jimmy and she were somehow fated to be together. Kate had spent her early years living with her father and mother in Chicago and their brownstone was next door to a stable where fire-fighting equipment was stored. When a fire was reported, a large bell outside the stable was rung to call the volunteer firefighters. To Kate, the alarm seemed to ring day and night. She found it extremely annoying and distracting. But one day as she was returning home, the fire bell rang, and the stable doors suddenly burst open. Out came a hand-pumped fire engine pulled by three large, white horses. The engine was painted a bright red and the brass work had been polished to a mirror finish which flashed in the sunlight.

Pedestrians scattered for their lives as the engine clattered down the street at a full gallop. Kate's jaw dropped as she watched the scene unfold. The fire engine had no seats, and the driver rode bareback on one of the horses. He kicked at the horse's flanks and urged ever greater speed, the horses' manes and his red hair streaming behind them. The fire engine tipped from side to side and seemed about to fall over at any time. But even with all the chaos of the moment, the driver's eyes and Kate's met before the fire engine disappeared around a corner. Kate could hear the driver give a laugh of pure exhilaration and then he was gone.

After that, whenever the fire alarm rang, Kate would rush to the living room windows to try and catch a glimpse of the dashing fireman. But for whatever reason, she never saw him again.

Until, that is, there was a knock on Kate's front door one Sunday afternoon. When she opened the door, there stood Jimmy, his hair freshly cut and holding a bouquet of flowers. They were married 2 months later.

Ten months after that, Jimmy was killed in a warehouse fire and Kate, with no means of support, applied for work with the Pinkertons.

Kate met the second man in her life at the Pinkerton Office in Chicago. He was a bear of a man named Timothy Webster, an English-born detective who was soon to play a major role in Pinkerton's spy service. He was everything Kate admired: well-educated, well-traveled and sophisticated. Kate was smitten the first time she met him.

They worked some minor cases together, sometimes posing as husband and wife. Love blossomed and Kate even began to imagine them having a life together. But their romance was complicated by the fact that Webster was married. Kate agonized over the morality of their affair, but she could not make herself break things off. However, sometimes fate makes the decisions for us that we cannot. In 1862, Webster was in Richmond posing as a member of a pro-Southern group while gathering information on the secessionist's plans and activities. But when Webster suddenly stopped sending reports, Pinkerton grew concerned and sent two Pinkerton detectives, Pryce Lewis, and John Scully, to Richmond to check on him.

As it turns out, Pinkerton's concern proved to be Webster's undoing. Webster had been suffering from inflammatory rheumatism but was recovering. But newly released Confederate operatives in Richmond recognized Lewis and Scully as Union spies and had them arrested. Scully eventually revealed information that led to Webster's arrest and trial for espionage.

In those days, most spies were not executed but rather held to be traded for important prisoners. But Webster's long-term success and deep infiltration was an embarrassment to the Confederacy, and they were determined he be hanged.

The hanging did not go well, and visions of the botched execution still haunt all who saw it. On the first attempt, the rope broke. When the guards helped him back on the scaffold, Webster was heard to say, 'I suffer a double-death!' He was killed on the second try.

Both men still came to Kate in her dreams. Not as much as they had in years past, but still with some frequency. The dreams always started out the same way, filling Kate's heart with joy as she held their faces in her hands, kissing their cheeks, lips, and eyes. Their voices were music, and their smiles lifted her soul to dizzying heights. But sooner or later she would awaken, quickly realizing that it was all a dream; grief would stab at her heart anew with an intensity little diluted from the day she first learned of their deaths. The pain was almost too much to bear.

A tear rolled down Kate's cheek as she lay there in the dark, exhausted. "Please," she begged of God, "no dreams tonight."

Merritt sat on a rocky beach next to the river. He lit his pipe and took a deep draw. There was only the slightest breeze and the smell of the river, a mixture of earth and fish, reminded Merritt of summers he had spent playing along the Scioto River outside of Columbus. He had taught Allen how to fish there just as Merritt's father had taught him. Tears began to well up in Merritt's eyes at the memory. *Stop*, he told himself. *Do not let the memory in.* For he knew that if he let one memory in, all would follow, and he would be overwhelmed.

Merritt willed himself to think instead about the day's meeting with Colonel Lowe. He felt a stirring deep inside, a building of anticipation. Colonel Lowe had confirmed much of what they knew about the ambush but—and most importantly—had also confirmed there was at least one person who had known the pay wagon's schedule in advance. There was no doubt in Merritt's mind that this was the man who had provided the schedule to the robbers. Merritt and Kate would find the man and learn the names of the robbers. The man would talk. Merritt would make sure that the man talked.

Merritt stared at the dark river. *And then what?* he asked himself. He knew he would kill them all or be killed trying. But if he succeeded, what feelings would replace the hatred that now lived in him? Or would he just perish, finally consumed by the dying embers of his own hate?

Merritt stood up and looked back at the rooming house. He thought about Kate. She was a handsome woman, charming and empathetic. But he sensed there was a core of steel within the silk and jasmine in which she often wrapped herself. And something deeper, as well. A great loss, a tragedy of some sort, he reckoned. When he caught her unawares, he sometimes saw a profound sadness tug at the corners of her mouth. *We are like two wounded animals*, he thought. *Given the chance, would we save or devour each other?*

But just as quickly as the thoughts about Kate came into his mind, guilt tried to push them away. Every notion he had that did not involve finding Allen's killers seemed somehow disloyal to his son. And to his wife Sadie.

Merritt had known Sadie McQueen his entire life. They had grown up next door to each other, and although Merritt was five years older than Sadie, they had become best friends. But it was inevitable, of course, that they would end up growing apart, if for no other reason than their age difference. Merritt regularly broke Sadie's heart when she saw him flirting with girls his own age and spending less and less time with her.

When Merritt left for West Point, he was a young man of eighteen and Sadie was just a girl of thirteen. But when Merritt returned home to Columbus after graduating, he discovered that something extraordinary had happened—Sadie had turned into a woman. And a very beautiful woman at that. Merritt was fatally smitten.

At first, Sadie feigned having no interest in the handsome young officer, although she later admitted she had known her whole life that they would someday marry. But Merritt pursued her endlessly, begging her to marry him before he was shipped off with the Army to Mexico. Whether he had simply worn her down, or she was finally convinced of his seriousness, Sadie said 'yes,' and they were married the same year.

Sadie had made a wonderful Army wife. She got along well with the other officer's wives and Merritt's superior officers adored Sadie. During the entire time Merritt remained in the Army, he never tired of seeing the other officers fighting for a chance to dance with Sadie. And they were not above pulling rank to do so. Merritt would begin a dance with Sadie and within moments another lieutenant was tapping him on the shoulder to cut in, quickly followed by a captain cutting in on him, then a major and so on. On one memorable night, Sadie made it all the way up to a Brigadier General in a single dance.

When Merritt decided to leave the military, Sadie was fully supportive. She had missed her friends and family back in Columbus and she disliked the many separations common to military service. So, they moved back to Ohio and Merritt joined his father in the banking business.

When Allen was born, Merritt had never been happier or more content in his life. *It was almost too perfect*, he thought, *making it too tempting for fate to step in and balance the scale*. And so it was. Two years after Allen's birth, Sadie caught a cold. Then things turned for the worse and within two weeks Sadie was dead. Pneumonia, the doctors had said.

Merritt had mourned Sadie, but the depth of his sense of loss was somewhat mitigated by the very existence of his son. Allen was noisily and cheerfully alive, bringing light to even the darkest regions of Merritt's soul.

"Oh, Sadie," Merritt said aloud. "Now I have lost the both of you and I do not know if I have the strength to move forward alone."

By the time Merritt returned to the rooming house, the sky had already begun to brighten in the east.

CHAPTER 7

Kitty and Isobel

Hemmingway wrote that "There is no hunting like the hunting of man, and those who have hunted armed men long enough and liked it, never care for anything else thereafter." But what Hemmingway did not mention was that chasing a man is one thing and catching him another. There is nothing more dangerous than a man who feels trapped or cornered. Most often he will turn to fight and there is always the danger that the hunters will become the hunted.

The only telegraph office in Dover was in the lobby of the Dover Hotel, the same building in which Colonel Lowe had his office. As Kate walked through the lobby, she once again saw the same junior officer sitting on the same sofa and, possibly, reading the same newspaper. As before, he paid her no attention. The door to the colonel's office was closed and Kate imagined him in there frantically pulling orders and requisitions out of one ever-growing pile and placing them on another.

The telegraph station consisted of a bank teller-like cage in the corner of the lobby in which a middle aged man with garters on his sleeves sat rapidly tapping out messages on a telegraph key.

When Kate cleared her throat to get his attention, he pointed her to a pad of paper forms and a pencil on the counter. "There, Missus," he said, not looking up. "Just fill out the form and leave it with the others in the outgoing basket."

"Ah, that is a problem," said Kate, lowering her voice. "This is most personal, and it would not do to leave a copy lying about. I was hoping that you would send my message and immediately return the text to me."

The man looked up at Kate from his telegraph key. "Surely, Missus, you can see the pile of messages waiting to be sent." The man glanced over in the direction of the colonel's office and lowered his own voice. "It would seem that the Army cannot go 10 minutes without ordering something, or canceling something, sometimes at the same time. I am sorry."

Kate gave the man a bright smile, then suddenly clutched her stomach and doubled-over. She gave out a cry of pain and grabbed the counter to support herself. The man rushed around the counter and held her arm. "Are you alright, Missus?" he asked.

Kate slowly straightened up and gave the man a weak smile. "It was just a kick."

"Oh? Oh!" said the man, suddenly understanding what she was implying. "Well, let me help you to a chair." But Kate just shook her head and said, "Thank you, but it would be best if I just got back to the boarding house."

The man nodded his head in understanding and whispered, "Just take a seat for a moment and I will send your telegram. The Army can hold their water for a bit." He helped Kate to a chair and then rushed back into his cage. A few minutes later, Kate's telegram had been sent and she carried the original document with her back to the rooming house:

The American Telegraph Co.

From   KITTY WARREN. DOVER TENN. JULY XXII.
To   ISOBEL MCQUEEN.C/O.THE SAUGANASH HOTEL.CHI-

CAGO ILL.

> AUNTIE ISOBEL. THE ARMY WILL NOT REVEAL TO
> ME THEIR INVESTIGATION OF COUSIN MICHAEL'S
> PENSION REQUEST. IF I AM TO ASSIST HIM, I RE-
> QUIRE THE NAME OF THE MAN/MEN THAT KNEW
> OF HIS DISCHARGE SCHEDULE. PLEASE ADVISE.
> LOVE KITTY

When Kate left the hotel, the young officer got up and walked over to the telegraph operator's cage. "What did she want?" he asked.

The telegraph operator looked up with a quizzical look on his face. "Who, Lieutenant Betron?"

"The woman who just left, you old fool."

"No need to be unpleasant, lieutenant, she just wanted to send a telegraph is all. Pretty little thing, preggers she is, nearly fainted right where you stand."

The lieutenant fought to keep his temper. "What did it say? The telegram?"

"Now, lieutenant, you know I ain't permitted to discuss such things! I could lose my job!"

Lieutenant Betron leaned over the counter and lowered his voice. "This is Army business. If you do not cooperate, I *guarantee* you will lose your job."

The telegraph operator sighed. "Jest so," he said. "Best I recall, she just told her Auntie she was trying to help some relative or other   with a pension."

"Did she give a name for this relative?"

"Michael or Matthew or something like that. Listen lieutenant, I send hundreds of telegrams every day..."

Lieutenant Betron rolled his eyes in frustration and walked into the cage. He began to sort through the pile of sent telegrams when the operator said, "It ain't there, lieutenant, she took it with her."

"Is that not unusual?"

The operator shrugged. "Some people do not like to leave a copy behind."

Lieutenant Betron walked out of the cage to return to the sofa. As he was leaving, he said, "I want to see anything else that woman sends or receives in return. Immediately. Is that understood?"

"Yes, lieutenant."

The next day, Kate and Merritt were sitting on the front porch of the rooming house when a boy came running up the sidewalk. When he saw Kate, he asked, "Miz Warren?" Kate nodded, tipped him, and anxiously ripped open the telegram he had been carrying.

Kate read it quickly and handed it to Merritt:

The American Telegraph Co.

From ISOBEL MCQUEEN.C/O.THE SAUGANASH HOTEL.CHICAGO ILL.

To KITTY WARREN. DOVER TENN. JULY XXIII.

> DEAREST NIECE. THE MAN YOU ARE SEEKING IS NAMED ALEXANDER LOVETT, WHO SERVED WITH COUSIN MATHEW. HOWEVER, HE MAY NO LONGER BE IN DOVER AS LAST I HEARD HE HAD LEFT THE ARMY. HE MAY HAVE RETURNED HOME TO NASHVILLE WHERE HIS FATHER IS A COOPER. LOVE, ISOBEL

Merritt smiled. "What?" Kate asked.

"Am I to assume that 'Isobel McQueen' is Allan Pinkerton?"

"It was his mother's maiden name," said Kate somewhat defensively. "We use it and the Sauganash Hotel address for messages we wish to keep anonymous."

Merritt had to look away from Kate. He had met Pinkerton once at a political event in Columbus during the War. Pinkerton was of average height, solidly built, with a thick brogue, a hot temper, and a penchant for single-malt scotch. *Few men*, thought Merritt, *would dare to call Allan Pinkerton 'Isobel' to his face.*

Kate waited until Merritt had composed himself, then said, "If you have had your moment of merriment, shall we discuss this new information?" Merritt wisely resisted the temptation to say 'Yes, Kitty," and motioned them towards the chairs on the porch. Out there, they had little chance of being overheard. They settled into two old rocking chairs in the shade next to the house wall.

Merritt made no effort to hide his excitement. "Once we find Lovett," he said, "we will be one step closer to finding the murderers of my son." Then he asked Kate to wait for a moment while he went back inside the rooming house. When he returned, he was carrying a bottle of sherry and 2 mis-matched glasses. He filled them and handed one to Kate. They touched glasses and Merritt said, "To the successful conclusion of our mission!"

"To our mission!" she said as she studied Merritt over the rim of her glass. He looked pale and unhealthy to her, thinner even then when she had met him just a few weeks before.

CHAPTER 8

Off to Nashville

Hold onto your miracle,
It's just a spark right now,
Guard it from the wind that blows,
Ignore the tongues that wag and the clock that drags so
slow,
Day to day the spark to a flame will grow,
On a day unexpected, the miracle in life will show
—Ann D'Silva, Sand & Sea: Footprints in the sand

Merritt and Kate left Dover early the next day. Not needing to do any exploring, they had the luxury of returning to Nashville by rail. Although most of Tennessee's railroads had been destroyed as the War raged across the state, the bulk of them had already been repaired. Their route was a bit circuitous as it first went north to Bowling Green, Kentucky, and then back south to Nashville, but it still provided a pleasant alternative to horseback riding in the searing summer heat.

Merritt and Kate sat in the club car sipping lemonade as the countryside passed by. Merritt found the rhythmic click-clack of the wheels both mesmerizing and soothing. His heartbeat soon synchronized to the cadence, and he felt a calm he had not known since he had learned of his son's death.

Merritt watched Kate as she wrote a report of her activities to Allan Pinkerton. Her brow furrowed as she concentrated, reminding Merritt of a schoolgirl doing her homework. Kate sensed him watching her and looked up. "What?" she asked.

Merritt smiled, embarrassed at being caught. "Nothing," he said. "You just reminded me of something."

Kate gave Merritt a bright smile and lay down her pencil. "Let me guess," she said. "I remind you of one of your spinster accountants doing her sums."

Merritt laughed and said, "Not at all, Mrs. Warne, but now you have put me in a difficult position."

"Oh, dear," said Kate. "How so?"

"How do I answer you without sounding forward, as I believe you to be neither a spinster nor anywhere near as ordinary as an accountant?" Merritt shook his head and smiled, "No, I do not find you ordinary at all."

Kate blushed. Not knowing what else to do, she reached for her pencil, returned to her report, and said, "You are very kind, Mr. Cowles."

After they had checked in at the St. Cloud hotel, Merritt and Kate retired to their separate rooms to unpack and prepare for dinner. As Kate bustled about, her thoughts went to Merritt. They had said nothing more of any real consequence after flirting in the club car. *We were flirting, were we not?* wondered Kate. Merritt confused her and, even if she would not admit it, flustered her. She had only three dresses with her, but she tried each one on at least four or 5 times before deciding on a simple purple silk dress with white piping on the sleeves. She believed it emphasized her thin waist, a feature of which she was quite vain. Then, at eight o'clock, Kate checked her hair in the mirror one last time and went downstairs to the dining room.

The dining room was all crystal, mirrors, and polished wood

with waiters in white gloves and black jackets. Kate looked elegant and beautiful, *princess-like*, thought Merritt. Every eye in the restaurant followed Merritt and her as they made their way to a table in back. Merritt—although he would never admit it —secretly enjoyed the envious looks from the other men in the dining room.

Merritt was in an expansive mood and insisted on ordering wine with dinner. Kate believed it was a little early in their journey to be celebrating, but she enjoyed seeing Merritt in such good spirits. Even his color looked better.

Kate tried to bring things back to the business between them and said, "Mr. Cowles, perhaps we should decide on how to proceed tomorrow..." But Merritt interrupted her by briefly touching her hand and it was like a shock went through her body.

"Please, Mrs. Warne, I would be honored if you would call me Merritt."

For a moment, Kate could say nothing. The sensation of Merritt's touch, however brief, had startled her. She had felt her whole body flush. She looked incredulously at Merritt. *Did you not feel that?* she wondered. But Merritt just sipped at his wine and waited for her reply. Finally, she said, "Of course, Merritt. And please call me Kate."

Merritt beamed at her. "Kate it is!" Their conversation was light, and Kate thought the dinner wonderful. Seemingly endless courses of food flowed in from the kitchen and Merritt would describe the various French wines that accompanied it. They talked about their childhoods and Merritt told wonderful, funny stories about growing up beside the Scioto River in Ohio. Kate laughed so much that tears sometimes ran down her cheeks.

Kate and Merritt were the last two people to leave the dining room that night.

Early the next morning, Merritt and Kate determined to go

looking for Alexander Lovett, which promised to be a challenge. Now that the War was over, control had been returned to the citizens of Nashville from the Union military, and it had become an eclectic and somewhat wild town. During the War, refugees— both southern and northern sympathizers as well as free blacks and escaped slaves—had poured into Nashville because jobs were plentiful in the warehouses and hospitals. It had a feeling of transience that it seemed to be in no hurry to lose.

Kate seemed unperturbed by the task. As she and Merritt left the hotel, she placed her arm through his and guided him down the street. They walked casually, seemingly without a clear destination, enjoying the sights and sounds of a city awakening.

Merritt said, "I confess to enjoying our walk, Kate, but should we not be looking for Mr. Lovett?"

"But we are," she said as she stopped in front of a newsstand. She turned to the proprietor and asked: "Do you have a copy of the most recent Nashville City Directory?"

"Let me check, Missus," the proprietor answered. He rooted around under his counter and then pulled out the latest he could find, dated 1860 to 1861. "Wonderful!" said Kate as she handed the man a dime. She thumbed through the paperback and quickly found what she was looking for. She held the page open and showed it to Merritt.

Merritt had to smile. "Is this something they teach you in Detective School?"

Kate smiled back. "Sometimes I get Lucky."

The Nashville City Directory was a listing of residents, streets, businesses, organizations, and institutions, giving their location. It was arranged alphabetically, and halfway down the 'Ls' was a listing for 'Lovett, Samuel, Occupation: Cooper, Address: 6 Peabody Street. There were other Lovetts but none whose profession was listed as a cooper.

"You think Samuel Lovett is Alexander's father?" Merritt asked.

Kate nodded. "A good bet. And even if Alexander is not staying with his father, his father may know where he is."

The City Directory also contained a street map which showed

Peabody Street running west from the Cumberland River towards the Union Railroad Depot. The low street number, six, indicated that the Lovett residence was at the end of the street near the river.

Merritt and Kate hired a hansom cab to travel to 6 Peabody Street. Although hansom cabs had been around since the 1830s, they were just becoming popular in the bigger cities. The cab seated two passengers and a driver who sat on a sprung seat behind the vehicle. The cab was painted a glossy black with gilded highlights and was pulled by a beautiful black Percheron horse. Even for two people, the cab was cozy, and Merritt was very conscious of Kate next to him, especially when bumps in the road would throw them together.

As they moved farther away from the city center, the neat brick townhouses and shops gave way to clapboard rowhouses interspersed with small manufacturing businesses and warehouses. A layer of black soot covered everything. Men and women walked along the sidewalks with their heads down, seemingly oblivious to everything around them.

A block away from 6 Peabody Street, the cab driver suddenly stopped. Merritt opened the hatch in the back of the cab roof and asked the driver if there was a problem. The driver pointed up the street to where a large number of people were gathered. "Some sort of mob up ahead," he said. "I do not reckon I care to go further. A rough neighborhood, this one is."

Merritt paid the driver, and the driver unlocked the cab doors to let them out. Merritt and Kate stepped out into the street, walking gingerly around horse droppings and trash and made their way to the sidewalks. The cab driver made a hasty U-turn and was quickly headed back the way he had come.

As Kate and Merritt approached the crowd, they saw a man lying in the street. There was a large butcher's knife lying near his hand and he was covered in blood from head to foot. There was also a trail of blood leading away from the body and into a nearby house. Merritt and Kate saw it at the same time: a crooked '6' painted on the doorframe. Six Peabody Street.

CHAPTER 9

The Death of Alexander Lovett

Three may keep a secret, if two of them are dead. —Benjamin Franklin

A bout 10 or 15 people stood around the body lying in the street. Merritt was not sure if they were curious or simply had nothing else to do. There certainly seemed to be no sense of urgency. Merritt turned towards one of the men and asked him, "Do you know this man?"

The man regarded Merritt for a moment and then walked away without saying anything. Merritt turned to Kate and said, "We seem a bit out of place here. Where are the police, I wonder?"

Kate looked over Merritt's shoulder and said, "They appear to be arriving now." Merritt turned and saw two men approaching, one with a flowing black beard and the other clean shaven. They were wearing what appeared to be blue surplus U.S. Army uniforms, but instead of slouch or Kepi hats, they wore stovepipe hats. Pinned on their chests were brass stars. Neither man appeared to be armed.

Both men were bruisers, their uniforms stretching tightly across their chests; they looked like they had been stevedores or meat packers before becoming constables. The people standing around suddenly began to drift away as the men approached.

But the police seemed only interested in Merritt and Kate. They barely even glanced at the body in the street.

The bearded man stood before Merritt and demanded, "Who are you?"

Merritt's face flushed with anger, but before he could say anything, the clean shaven policeman gently pushed his partner back away from Merritt. "Sorry, Sir," he said to Merritt. He told the other policeman to go guard the body and then tipped his hat to Kate. "I am Officer Ferguson," he said with a soft brogue, "and that is Officer O'Connor. We cannot help but wonder what two people of yer station are doing here in this neighborhood. 'Tis a dangerous place at best, and then there is the matter of him," he said, indicating the dead man.

"We came seeking a man named Alexander Lovett," said Merritt. "We believe his father lives at 6 Peabody Street."

"Well, it appears you have found him. The son, that is. The father died some months ago. That is Alex lying there. He is well known to us, 'though we did not know he had returned to Nashville. We thought him still in the Army."

Merritt glanced at the body then back to the policeman. "May we examine the body?"

"Now, Sir, there I have to draw the line as this is police business. But perhaps you can tell me why you and the Missus was looking for poor Alex?"

Kate stepped towards Officer Ferguson and pulled out her Pinkerton identification card and badge. She held them up before his eyes. The policeman scanned them quickly as Officer O'Connor walked up to them. "What is going on?" O'Connor asked.

"They are Pinkertons," answered Ferguson. Then, almost to himself, "Wonder what kinda business Alex got hisself into this time."

Kate said, "Mr. Lovett is a suspect in an armed robbery in which several people were killed."

Officer Ferguson's eyes grew wide. "Alex was a petty thief, charged a few times with assault, mostly from bar fights. But I never thought him truly violent."

Kate reached into her purse and pulled out a small pad of paper and a pencil. "Tell you what I will do, Officer Ferguson. If you would like, I will keep you updated on our investigation into Mr. Lovett's death and of any subsequent developments. In return, perhaps you can share with us your knowledge of this area and the Lovetts. I believe it could benefit us both to work together." Kate handed the policeman a piece of paper with her name and telegraph address in Chicago written on it.

Officer Ferguson gave Kate a big smile. "Yes, it could be very beneficial," he said. His mind was spinning. He already had visions of himself being handed a certificate of honor and a promotion to detective if he solved the murder—with the help of the Pinkertons, of course. He could hardly wait to get home and tell his wife.

"May we examine the body?" Kate asked.Ferguson nodded and said, "Of course!" He led Merritt and Kate to Alexander Lovett, then moved aside. Kate stepped carefully around the body, trying to avoid stepping in the blood and gore.

"So much blood!" Merritt exclaimed. "Good Lord, how many times was he stabbed?"

Lovett was lying half on his side, face up, one arm pinned beneath his body. It was one of those awkward positions that only the dead can seem to manage. Fighting a visceral reaction to the carnage, Kate reached down and pushed his vest aside with her pencil. "I see no stab wounds at all," she answered. She looked for something with which to clean the pencil, but finding nothing, she threw the pencil away. "I see several bullet wounds: two in the arm that is exposed, one in the thigh and at least two in the chest. There may be more I cannot see beneath all the blood."

Officer Ferguson stood behind her, madly writing notes in a small notebook that police often carry. "He died hard," he said. Kate nodded in agreement and turned to the butcher knife. It was covered with blood. But there was no way to tell if it was Lovett's blood or someone else's.

While Kate, Merritt and Officer Ferguson were examining the

body, Officer O'Connor had followed the blood trail into 6 Peabody Street. Moments later, he ran back out into the street calling for Officer Ferguson. He was drained of color and his eyes were wide. He pointed to the house and said, almost in a whimper, "There. In there."

Merritt was the first of the three to enter the small clapboard house. Officer O'Connor waited outside. Merritt had not taken two steps into the hallway when he let out a gasp. Blood was everywhere, great pools of it on the floor, dripping from the walls, and even the ceilings. There were long arcs of blood spatter everywhere, like the work of a mad artist. In the middle of it all, lay another body, a pistol lying by its side.

The copper smell of blood, gunpowder and corruption was nearly overwhelming. Flies seemed to be everywhere; one could see them dancing on the corpse, gorging themselves, licking blood from their legs and sucking it in through their proboscises. Kate covered her mouth and nose with a handkerchief and shuddered with revulsion when flies would land on her hands or face. She forced herself to kneel next to the body. The cause of death was not hard to determine. The man had been slashed so viciously that Kate could see white ribs through the blood, and he was almost decapitated. Kate had had enough. She stood up and rushed out the door, followed closely by Merritt and Officer Ferguson.

Outside, they took deep breaths of the fresh air. After a time, Kate asked Officer Ferguson if he knew the victim inside the house. Ferguson shook his head 'no,' and turned to Officer O'Connor, who was sitting on the curb. "You know him, Lad?" O'Connor shook his head but did not look up. The murder scene had deeply affected them all. Even Merritt, who had seen combat during the war with Mexico, was shocked by the sheer brutality of it.

CHAPTER 10

Herbert Steinkraus

Allies never trust each other, but that doesn't spoil their effectiveness. –Ayn Rand

Merritt and Kate once again sat in the dining room of the St. Cloud Hotel, but this time there was no preening, no light banter or furtive glances. Merritt slouched in his chair and sipped morosely from his whiskey. "Do you think it coincidence that Lovett was killed just as we began to look for him?" he asked Kate.

"I do not believe in coincidences," she answered. "Fate, perhaps, but not coincidence."

Merritt nodded his understanding and signaled the waiter for another drink. "It seemed pretty obvious to me that Lovett killed his own assassin. It is unfortunate that neither of the police officers recognized him."

"I will keep in touch with the police. It is always possible that they may identify the assassin later."

"About that," Merritt said. "I was surprised when you offered Officer Ferguson your collaboration."

Kate smiled and said, "Relations with the local authorities are always difficult. If they believe we Pinkertons are out solely for our own glory, they may conceal key pieces of evidence. Things usually work out best if Pinkerton resources are combined with local knowledge and credit shared."

"So where now?"

"I have been thinking about this all day," answered Kate. "If we eliminate coincidence, then the robbers must have known we were looking for Lovett. But how?"

"The only people who knew we were looking for him was us and Allan Pinkerton." Merritt's eyes suddenly grew wide. "And..."

"And the telegraph operator," Kate finished.

After a hurried trip back to Dover, Tennessee, Kate and Merritt once again sat on the front porch of the little boarding house as a summer afternoon thunderstorm passed through. The wind howled and the rain blew sideways for a few minutes, and then it was done. *Much ado about nothing*, thought Kate. But it did reduce the humidity and drop the temperature a bit, at least for a little while.

Kate loved the electric smell of the air during a thunderstorm and the stray, refreshing raindrops that found their way under the porch roof. Thunderstorms always reminded Kate of her childhood. Her parents were stoic and strict and gave her little comfort during storms; but her grandfather would let her crawl up into his lap and he would speak to her in soothing tones until the storms had passed.

Kate and Merritt had been back in Dover for 4 days. Each day, they had taken turns discretely watching the Dover Hotel, seeking to learn the telegraph operator's routine. It varied little. They learned that the man's name was Herbert Steinkraus. Steinkraus would arrive at work precisely at 7:00 a.m. At noon, he would eat his lunch from a greasy paper bag at his station. He never left the Hotel during the day. At 7:00 p.m., he would walk to a small cottage on the outskirts of Dover where he appeared to live alone.

As the thunder faded off into the distance, Merritt checked

his pocket watch. "It is nearly 6:30," he said to Kate. Kate nodded and stood up. She took a small derringer out of a pocket in her jacket, checked the load, and carefully replaced it. She and Merritt stepped off the porch and began the 10-minute walk to Steinkraus' cottage.

Both Merritt and Kate were dressed in clothes that did not make them stand out. Kate wore a casual dress that any local woman might wear, and Merritt wore pants with suspenders over a white collarless shirt and a soft hat. They looked neither indigent nor affluent.

When they reached Steinkraus' cottage, they found the door unlocked and they let themselves in. As their eyes adjusted to the dim light, they saw it was neat and clean, with pillows and knickknacks that suggested a woman's touch. They were concerned for a moment that Steinkraus might not live alone until they saw a daguerreotype on a table, draped in black ribbon. The woman in the picture had her lips pursed, making her look stern and unapproachable.

The cottage was all one floor with no dividers. In one corner there was a bed, a small kitchen in another, and a sitting area in the third. The sitting area contained a well-worn armchair and little else; the kitchen was furnished with a small table and 2 chairs. Merritt placed the kitchen chairs side-by-side facing the door where he and Kate sat waiting for Steinkraus to return.

By quarter after 7:00, Steinkraus had still not returned. Both Merritt and Kate were becoming concerned that somehow, they had been given away when the door opened, and Herbert Steinkraus walked in. He was carrying a paper sack with a loaf of bread protruding from it. Because of the dim light, Steinkraus did not see Merritt and Kate right away. He closed the door behind him and was walking to the kitchen when he noticed them. He threw the sack to the ground and started to run for the door. "Do Not," said Kate.

Steinkraus froze in place and slowly turned to face Kate and Merritt. Kate motioned Steinkraus to the armchair with her derringer. Steinkraus gave out a deep sigh and slumped into the chair. "I knew it," he said.

Merritt looked at Steinkraus. "Knew what?" he asked.

Steinkraus looked from Merritt to Kate and back to Merritt again. "Ain't this about the telegrams?"

When Merritt nodded, Steinkraus dropped his eyes from Merritt's. "I knew it," he said again.

Merritt gave out a sigh of frustration. "Again, Mr. Steinkraus, you knew what?"

"I knew I was gonna lose my job. I told the lieutenant, but he did not care. He said it was Army business and that if I did not show him the telegrams the Army would fire me anyway."

Merritt and Kate exchanged a glance. "Lieutenant who?" Merritt asked.

"Betron. Lieutenant Betron. He is Colonel Lowes aide. You probably seen him in the Hotel lobby."

Merritt and Kate spent the next hour questioning Steinkraus about the telegrams as well as the activities of both Colonel Lowe and Lieutenant Betron. When she believed they could learn no more, Kate stepped in front of Steinkraus and showed him her Pinkerton badge. "Now, Mr. Steinkraus, I cannot emphasize enough right now how much trouble you are in. You are not only in danger of losing your job but of going to jail as well. Do you understand me?"

Steinkraus, wide-eyed, nodded. "Yes, Missus."

"But there may be a way around this for you..."

"Anything," Steinkraus interrupted.

"Are you a patriot, Mr. Steinkraus?"

Steinkraus looked surprised by the question. "Yes, Missus, 'though I was too old to fight in the past Rebellion. But I thought I could do my part by sending telegrams for the Army."

Kate studied Steinkraus for a moment, then turned to Merritt. "What do you think?"

Merritt was not sure where Kate was going, but he played along. "Mr. Steinkraus seems basically trustworthy to me. I can see where Lieutenant Betron put him between a rock and a hard place."

"Very well," said Kate as she turned back to Steinkraus. "Let me lay it out plainly for you, Mr. Steinkraus. You now work for us. First, you must tell no one what happened here tonight. Second, you will continue to do as Betron asks; however, you will relay to me, in person or via a telegraph address I will give you, any new instructions he gives you. And lastly, you will willingly perform any task I ask of you."

"And if I do these things, I will not go to jail?"

Kate nodded. "So long as you do what I ask of you. But if I find you are lying to me or working against me, you will never see another day as a free man."

Steinkraus grew pale. "Yes, Missus."

As Kate and Merritt walked back to their boarding house, Kate once again took his arm. Merritt smiled at her, his good mood restored by the information they had obtained. "Do you think Steinkraus will do as we asked?"

Kate shrugged her shoulders. "It all depends," she answered, "of whom Mr. Steinkraus is more afraid, Lieutenant Betron or us."

"And now?"

"And now we wait to see what develops."

CHAPTER 11

August 30, 1865

The Colonel and the Lieutenant

Nobody is a villain in their own story. We're all the heroes of our own stories. —George R. R. Martin

Colonel Augustine Hollingsworth (Ret.), late of the Army of the Potomac, veteran of the Mexican War and a hero of Shiloh, leaned back in his chair, his feet up on the porch railing. He was not sleeping, exactly, more like daydreaming. He had his planter's hat pulled down over his eyes and he breathed in deeply, enjoying the scent of hyacinth and lemon blossoms that perfumed the air.

The colonel was suddenly brought back to the present by a small hand shaking him. A child's voice said, "Sir colonel, this came for you from Key West."

The colonel swung his feet off the railing and turned towards the child, a young boy of around 11-years-old named 'Sammy.' Sammy's parentage was unknown, he just seemed to come with the island. He was there when the colonel and his men arrived, and the colonel suspected Sammy would stay there when they left. The colonel took a telegram from him and patted him on the head. "Thank you, Sammy."

When the boy was gone, the colonel opened the telegram:

The American Telegraph Co.

From   F B. DOVER TENN.AUGUSTXXX.
To   A H.C/O.LESTER VERNON ESQ.KEYWEST FL.
      THE LEASE HAS BEEN TERMINATED.SOME PROP   ERTY
DAMAGE.AWAIT   FURTHER   INSTRUCTIONS.YOUR   SERVANT,
ETC.

Colonel Hollingsworth folded the telegraph and put it in his pocket. *'Some property damage'? What the hell does that mean?* He got up from his chair and walked into the cottage. He sat at his writing desk, scratched and scarred from years in the field, and began to write:

To: Lieutenant Frank Betron, Fort Donelson, Tenn
From: Daddy
Message: Come home immediately.

The colonel folded the paper and placed it in his pocket. He got up and walked outside. The cottage was part of a small compound cut into the palms, palmetto bushes and scrub brush. There was another smaller cottage where his staff slept and a few small outbuildings. The colonel followed a well-worn path that ran from his cottage down a slight hill to a wooden dock where a flat-bottomed work skiff and a small sailboat were moored.

Sitting in the shade of a large palm tree was a man cradling a rifle. He was shirtless in the heat and his skin glistened with sweat. He jumped to his feet when he saw Colonel Hollingsworth approaching. "Colonel!" he said, snapping to attention.

"At ease, Earl! You ain't in the Army anymore." The colonel looked around. "Where is Bear?" he asked.

Earl shrugged his shoulders. "Do not know, colonel. Prob'ly home taking a nap."

Colonel Hollingsworth frowned. He had tried many times to talk to Bear—whose real name in Seminole was No-go-see—

about his duties at the compound. But Bear would just smile and shrug his shoulders. And it was not just the Seminoles who lived life unhurried in the tropical heat; it seemed that the high temperatures and draining humidity affected everyone and anyone who spent any time in the Keys, sapping energy and ambition alike.

The colonel handed the folded paper to Earl and said, "Find Bear and have him take this to the telegraph office in Key West." As Earl turned to leave, the colonel said, "And send Cyril to me. He is in the cottage."

When Earl left, the colonel took Earl's spot in the shade. There was just the lightest breeze blowing in off the little inlet. The colonel removed his hat and wiped his brow with a bright red bandana, then leaned back against the palm tree. He thought about the mysterious telegram from the lieutenant. Clearly, something had gone wrong. That, in itself, did not bother the colonel too much. He had long ago learned that in combat the best plans fell apart the moment the first shot is fired. But he felt blinded by being so far away, unable to see new developments in time to take some corrective action.

Colonel Hollingsworth stood up and began to walk back to his cottage. It was time for the lieutenant to get out of Dover.

Herbert Steinkraus took off his headphones and carried a telegram over to where Lieutenant Betron sat on the sofa reading. "This just came in for you," he said.

The lieutenant did not bother to look up. "Who is it from?"

"Your Daddy," answered Steinkraus.

The lieutenant looked up, wide-eyed. "My Daddy?" He grabbed the telegram out of Steinkraus' hands and read it quickly. "Sumbitch!" he exclaimed. After a moment, he looked up at Steinkraus and said, "You tell no one about this, understand?"

Steinkraus nodded and walked back to his cage.

Lieutenant Betron threw his newspaper aside. He felt vaguely guilty, as if he had done something wrong and was being called to account. But the botched assassination was not his fault and at least Lovett had been eliminated. Anyway, he had remained in Dover only to keep an eye on the military investigation for the colonel. It was probably best if he moved on. A smile pulled at his lips as the lieutenant thought about the money owed to him. Soon, very soon, he would head to Mexico where he would spend it on fine whiskey and brown-eyed girls.

The lieutenant walked out of the hotel and headed for his boarding house. He thought briefly about telling Colonel Lowe he was leaving and resigning his commission. After all, that would be the honorable thing to do. The lieutenant had to laugh at himself: *Honor? This is no time for self-delusion. I am a thief now and a killer of innocent men. No, I resigned my commission a long time ago.*

When the lieutenant reached his room, he began packing his belongings in an old rucksack. He owned little. A dress uniform hung in the armoire along with a few pairs of civilian pants and shirts. He took off his uniform and threw it in a corner of the armoire, then dressed himself in civilian clothes. After packing his service revolver and a few toilet articles, the lieutenant was ready to leave.

That night, he was on a train headed for Mobile Bay.

CHAPTER 12

In Dover- September 1, 1865

At the first kiss I felt something melt inside me that hurt in an exquisite way. All my longings, all my dreams and sweet anguish, All the secrets that slept deep within me came awake, everything was transformed and enchanted, everything made sense. —Hermann Hesse

Merritt and Kate strolled around the small town of Dover. It was one of those beautiful summer evenings that can be magical, the kind that make the old feel young again and the young feel the pull of infinite possibilities. There were few lights on in the little town, and no streetlights to hide the stars; the Milky Way glowed and twinkled like a river of light. Merritt was overly conscious of the feel of Kate's arm through his, and the scent she wore made his head swim. He looked at her out of the corner of his eyes and wondered at her beauty. Here she was, dressed as plainly as a shopkeeper's wife, and yet she seemed even more beautiful than she had in Nashville. How was that possible?

Merritt slowed his gait, hoping to extend their walk. He could not deny his growing feelings for Kate. But two emotions continued to pull at him, one against the other: guilt and—what? — hopefulness? Not that long ago, he lived only to kill the men that had murdered his son. That had not changed, but now he was beginning to think there could be something more.

Kate looked at Merritt and asked, "Did you say something?"

Merritt shook his head. "I was just thinking what a beautiful night it is."

Kate squeezed his arm. "I remember nights like this when I was a little girl: stars so close it seemed as though you could grab them by the handful."

Merritt stopped walking and turned toward Kate. He sensed a moment had come and if he did not take it, it might be lost to him forever. He pulled Kate to him, and when she did not protest, he kissed her. Neither of them moved, and it is unclear how long they might have stood there until a voice came from the bushes, "Where have you two been? I have already been to your boarding house twice looking for you!"

Startled, Kate turned towards the voice. "Mr. Steinkraus?"

Merritt and Kate sat at Steinkraus' little kitchen table while the telegraph operator paced around the small cottage, glancing nervously at the windows and the front door. "If Lieutenant Betron has indeed left town," said Kate, "I think you have little to fear, Mr. Steinkraus."

Steinkraus sighed and sat down heavily in his armchair. "I hope you are right, Missus."

Kate glanced again at copies of the two telegrams Steinkraus had provided them. Merritt and she had already read them several times. They both were between 'A.H.' and 'F.B.' It seemed a fair assumption that 'F.B.' was Lieutenant Frank Betron, but 'A.H.' was unknown to them. Kate looked up at Steinkraus. "Do you know who this 'A.H.' is?" she asked. "Or Lester Vernon, Esq.?"

Steinkraus shook his head. "I do not know anyone with the initials 'A.H.' Nor do I know any lawyer named 'Lester Vernon.' But it ain't uncommon for people to send telegrams to different places to hold for them. Hotels, lawyers, restaurants, whatever.

Why, I remember one gentleman used to receive all his mail and telegrams care of a brothel in New Orleans..."

"Do you know if Lieutenant Betron had sent or received any telegrams from A. H. before?" Kate interrupted.

Steinkraus shook his head again. "I am sorry, Missus, but I do not recall any other telegrams to or from any A.H."

Kate nodded and turned to Merritt. "Still," she said, "it is obvious that A.H., whoever he is, was not happy with Lieutenant Betron's report of 'property damage' occurring during the 'lease termination.'" Kate shrugged her shoulders: "Bad luck for them that the assassin was killed and might lead us back to them; bad luck for us he succeeded in killing Lovett."

Merritt picked up the two telegrams and placed then in his pocket. As they stood up to leave, Kate walked over to Steinkraus and said, "Thank you, Mr. Steinkraus, for doing your duty." She handed him a carte de visite on which she had written the address of the Pinkerton Office in Chicago. "Should Lieutenant Betron reappear in Dover, or should you discover any new information that might help us, please telegram me care of this address."

Steinkraus jumped to his feet. "Thank you, Missus, and best of luck to you and your baby." Merritt, who was just walking out the front door, stopped and spun around. Seeing the look on Merritt's face, Kate grinned and looked quickly away. "Why thank you, Mr. Steinkraus!" She lowered her voice to a stage whisper and added, "You might be interested to know that I am considering the name 'Herbert' is it is a boy. That is a fine name, is it not?" Steinkraus' smile lit the room.

Merritt and Kate walked back to their boarding house in an awkward silence. One kiss and their relationship had changed and neither of them knew how to deal with it. Kate stopped walking and turned to face Merritt. "I think we need to discuss what happened between us tonight," she said. When Merritt did not respond, she continued: "I do not know if we can go on working together, Merritt. Our mission requires us to maintain a degree of professionalism that may no longer be possible."

Merritt stood looking at her, expressionless. "I had the same thought," he said.

Kate looked shocked. "You did?"

Merritt nodded. "I did," he said. Then he reached for Kate and pulled her to him. Just before he kissed her, he said, "It was one of my less intelligent ideas."

Back on the porch of the boarding house, Merritt and Kate sat again in the old rockers sipping sherry. He gave Kate a serious look and asked, "Should you be drinking that?"

For a moment, Kate was not sure what Merritt meant. Then, "Oh, very funny! Bad for the baby, do you think?"

Merritt smiled. "I must admit you had me going there for a moment."

Kate smiled sweetly at him. "Why, Merritt, what do you mean?"

Merritt laughed and covered Kate's hand with his own. She felt herself blush at his touch. "Is this the 'new professionalism,' Mr. Cowles?" she asked.

Merritt gave Kate a wide-eyed look. "Why, Kate, does my mere proximity befuddle you? Need we work separately and from different wings of the house?"

Kate smiled and pulled her hand back. "My, you do have a high opinion of yourself. One kiss and..."

"Two kisses," interrupted Merritt.

"Oh, never mind," said Kate, faking exasperation. "Back to business, Merritt. When do we leave?"

"For the Keys? I have booked us train tickets to Mobile and then a steamer to Key West. We leave tomorrow at 9:00 a.m."

Merritt and Kate did not realize it, but they were taking exactly the same route as Lieutenant Breton and were only one day behind him.

CHAPTER 13

Key West- September 1865

The West Indian is not exactly hostile to change, but he is not much inclined to believe in it. This comes from a piece of wisdom that his climate of eternal summer teaches him. It is that, under all the parade of human effort and noise, today is like yesterday, and tomorrow will be like today; that existence is a wheel of recurring patterns from which no one escapes; that all anybody does in this life is live for a while and then die for good, without finding out much; and that therefore the idea is to take things easy and enjoy the passing time under the sun... —Herman Wouk

After a two-hour boat ride, Cyril Winebrenner made his way through Key West to Thomas Street. He got lost several times, which did little to improve his mood; he was a northern boy by birth, and he detested the tropical heat. He stopped in the shade of a large bush and rechecked the colonel's note: Lester Vernon, Esq. 18B, Thomas Street. Few buildings in Key West bothered with street numbers and Cyril had to work backwards from one of the few that did. Eighteen Thomas Street appeared to be a two-story building with offices on both floors. The ground floor office window had 'Dentist' in flaking gold letters, so Cyril assumed 18B must be the second floor.

Cyril climbed the stairs and stopped to catch his breath when he reached the upper landing. He was grossly overweight, and he was sweating profusely through his woolen suit. No one could convince him to buy linen clothes for some relief from the tropical heat; he was saving every penny for his new life in Canada. He thought about the cabin he had purchased in Saskatchewan and imagined the cool days and nights that awaited him. *I should be there now*, he thought morosely. But the colonel had asked them all to remain in Key West until they were sure the Army investigation was not closing in on them. 'Do you want to spend the rest of your lives looking back over your shoulders?' the colonel had asked. And there were loose ends to tie up.

Cyril opened the glass door marked 'Lester Vernon, Esq.,' and entered the small vestibule that served as a reception area. There were two uncomfortable-looking wooden chairs and a desk behind which a plain, grey-haired woman sat. She looked up and smiled when Cyril walked in. "May I help you?" she asked.

Cyril smiled back. "Is Mr. Vernon in?"

"He is. May I ask what this is about?"

"A little unfinished business," Cyril answered. "I will let myself in."

The receptionist jumped up from her chair and tried to intercept Cyril. "Sir, wait, please!" But Cyril had already opened the office door. In two strides, he was at the lawyer's desk. When Lester Vernon rose from his chair in protest, Cyril pulled a pistol from his jacket, placed it against the lawyer's chest and pulled the trigger. The lawyer's body muffled most of the sound of the shot.

Behind him, Cyril heard the receptionist scream. He turned around and casually pointed his pistol at her forehead. Her eyes grew wide, but before she could scream again, he pulled the trigger. This shot, unmuffled, seemed inordinately loud in the small office.

Cyril walked back into the reception area and sat in one of the chairs, which creaked under his weight. He held his pistol in his lap as he waited to see if anyone came running in to investigate. Cyril was aware that his large size made him memorable, and he would leave no witnesses to identify him. After a few minutes, when no one appeared, Cyril got up and left the office. He walked down the stairs and headed back to the harbor where the Seminole called Bear was waiting to take him back to the colonel's compound.

That evening, Colonel Hollingsworth and his men sat outside in the relatively cool air. Even after the sun set, the temperature drop was modest. The colonel and Lieutenant Betron sat on rockers on the front porch while Cyril and Earl sat on the porch steps. "We are now four," said the colonel. "As you have no doubt heard by now, Joe Jackett was killed in his attempt to eliminate Lovett before he could be questioned by the Army about the payroll schedule. Killed each other, apparently."

Earl Hassler shook his head. "Lovett musta been a tough sumbitch. Ain't many men who could fight Joe Jackett to a draw." The men all nodded, and Earl added, "'Course, that does simplify the math a bit. Dividing the loot four ways instead'a 5, I mean."

Cyril gave out a low growl and said, "Perhaps I can simplify it more, Earl. Make the split three ways instead'a 4, I mean."

Earl paled. He had forgotten that Joe Jackett had served alongside Cyril in the War and had been one of Cyril's only friends. "Sorry, Cyril, I was just makin' a joke is all."

The colonel raised his hands for quiet and said, "Now Boys, I regret the death of every one of our comrades. But sometimes a sacrifice needs to be made for the greater good. Each of these deaths, as regrettable as they are, has distanced us more from the Army's investigation. We may soon be able to go our separate ways, confident that our 'retirements' will be long, peaceful and uninterrupted."

"Soon?" asked Cyril, his disappointment obvious. "I thought

the lawyer was the last connection between us and the robbery."

The colonel glanced briefly at Lieutenant Betron and said, "There is a new development. There was a man and woman up in Dover who went to see Colonel Lowe. What they discussed we do not know, but the woman received a telegram a day later with Lovett's name and location in it. We have reason to believe that they subsequently went looking for Lovett in Nashville. Fortunately, Mr. Lovett had predeceased their visit."

As they stepped off the steamer, Merritt and Kate were blinded by the sunlight and their senses assaulted by the climate; the September heat and humidity seemed to form a gossamer curtain through which Key West danced and shimmered. "Dear Lord!" said Merritt. "Is it always this hot here?"

Kate started to respond when she noticed a man weaving through the people on the crowded wharf. He was heading straight for Kate and Merritt, never taking his eyes off them. Merritt saw the man too, and he moved his hand closer to the pistol he wore in a shoulder holster under his jacket. The man showed them his empty hands as he neared them. He nodded at Merritt and asked, "Missus Warne?" When Kate nodded, the man said, "My name is Borrelli. I work for the Agency." Borrelli looked around and asked, "Do you mind if we step away from the crowd?"

Merritt studied the man as they walked to a quieter place on the wharf. He was of average height, clean-shaven with dark hair. He was wearing light linen clothing, a straw hat, and a pair of 'verres de cocquille,' grey-tinted glasses favored by Civil War soldiers to protect against sunlight during long marches. When they were away from the throng, Borrelli said, "I was working another case here in Key West when I got a telegram three days ago from Mr. Pinkerton. He asked me to keep an eye on a lawyer named Vernon until you and Mr. Cowles arrived. However, the request from Mr. Pinkerton came too late."

"Vernon has left town?" Kate asked.

Borrelli shook his head. "No, he was murdered." Kate and Merritt stared at Borrelli, speechless. Borrelli handed Kate a card on which he had printed the name of a boarding house in Key West. "I know nothing more. But I have some contacts in the local constabulary. Should I learn anything useful about Mr. Vernon's death, I will let you know. In the meantime, if there is anything I can do for you, just ask." Kate and Merritt thanked Borrelli and watched morosely as he turned and made his way back through the crowd. When Borrelli had disappeared from sight, Merritt gathered up their luggage. "Dammit," he said, "it seems we are always one step behind."

Merritt and Kate had made little progress away from the wharf when they were suddenly surrounded by a group of men, hats in hand, who asked if they could carry their luggage for them. The men were of different ages and sizes, but the one thing they all had in common was their obvious destitution; they were unshaven and unwashed and stunk of cheap rum and wine. Merritt selected two of the largest men and gratefully handed over the two suitcases he was carrying. The other men were turning to walk away when Merritt surprised them by giving them each a few coins. "Thank you, Mister," they said. "Bless you, Sir."

Kate, who had been to Key West before, had recommended they book rooms at *The Fleming Inn* at the corner of Fleming Street and Simonton, a few blocks in from the docks. Unlike Nashville, there were no hansom cabs here, so they walked. As they proceeded—Merritt in front, Kate behind him shaded by a bright pink parasol and the two men following—Merritt noticed how the appearance of Key West changed as soon as they left the waterfront. Gone were the sailors' bars and the stench of coal and kerosene, replaced by neat little cottages surrounded by gardens filled with tropical flowers. Shops along the way offered products from all over the world, from French silk fabrics to English crystal. Merritt turned to Kate and said, "I had no idea Key West was so prosperous!"

Kate smiled. "It is no secret that Key West grew rich plundering wrecks along her reefs. Everything from Spanish Galleons to Confederate blockade runners to unlucky freighters." Lowering her voice, Kate added, "But some suspect that many of the ships were intentionally lured to their doom by misleading navigation signals from land. But I do not suggest that you voice such theories at any local establishment where liquor is served."

Merritt's eyes grew wide. *Spanish treasure!* There is a little boy at the core of most men, and Merritt had heard little Kate had said after 'Spanish Galleons.' Visions of pirates and piles of gold coins filled his imagination. "They have found Spanish gold here?" he asked?

"Tonight, I will introduce you to a man who bathes in Spanish gold and drapes his wife in pirate booty. He is one of the richest men in Key West."

Merritt looked at Kate suspiciously. "Now I think you are teasing me."

Kate just smiled and twirled her parasol. "Oh, ye of little faith," she said.

CHAPTER 14

An Evening with Captain Castor

"He'sh mad?"
"Sort of mad. But mad with lots of money."
"Ah, then he can't be mad. I've been around; if a man hash lotsh of money he'sh just ecshentric." —Terry Pratchett

T he Fleming Inn occupied two acres. It was hidden from view by lush shrubbery and the grounds were criss-crossed by foot paths. Raised planters filled with orchids, Gulf Coast Lupine, Swamp Sunflowers, and wild Pennyroyal lined the main path along with several small koi ponds. Merritt could see why Kate had recommended the Inn; it was lush, tranquil and the abundant foliage cooled and per-fumed the air.

The Inn was a simple, pink, two-story stucco building which held six rooms on the second floor and a dining room on the first. The windows were floor-to-ceiling and adorned with or-nate woodworking. In every guest room, large French doors opened on to a private balcony.

After they had unpacked, it was nearly 6:00 p.m. and they rushed to prepare themselves for the evening. Kate had told Mer-ritt they were going to have dinner with an old friend of hers, a Captain William Castor, and his wife Viola. Captain Castor, according to Kate, knew everyone in Key West and perhaps the entire chain of keys as well.

Merritt had dressed as Kate had recommended in 'tropical casual,' which was white shirt and trousers and a light linen jacket. He wore no tie, which he found refreshing. After all, he had worn a coat and tie to work nearly every day for over 25 years. Kate was wearing a blue and white print, cotton dress. In the style of the times, the dress had dropped shoulders, a fitted bodice, a full skirt, and long bishop sleeves. Not that Merritt would understand or care about any of these style points; to him, Kate's beauty surpassed the need for any physical adornment.

"Now let me tell you a little about Captain Castor," Kate said as they strolled arm-in-arm the few blocks to a restaurant called 'The Crow's Nest' on Greene Street. "The good captain started out as a common sailor, saved his money and bought a sloop, then, over the years, a fleet of sloops. He became a wealthy man."

"Classic rags-to-riches," said Merritt, "a real Horatio Alger story."

"Ah, but there is more. Remember when I mentioned wreck salvaging earlier? Most anyone in the Keys with a boat at least dabbles in it. Well, several years ago, Captain Castor was salvaging a Confederate blockade runner that had run aground on one of what are called the 'Key West Gulfside reefs.' There are three or four of them and I do not remember which held the shipwreck, but the point of the story is what he found *under* the wreck."

Merritt stopped walking and turned to Kate. "Under?"

"As Captain Castor tells it, there was little in the wrecked blockade runner to salvage; either someone else had beaten him to her or she had long since lost her cargo to the waves and current. They had just decided to move on when one of his divers emerged from the water carrying an object that sparkled in the sun, casting bright spots of light which danced around the ship. The entire crew gathered around the man and gasped when he held the object high: it was a thick gold chain to which was attached a large diamond pendant. The diamond, according to the captain, was the size of a cricket ball. Just by happenstance, the blockade runner had settled on top of the grave of a Spanish galleon which had sunk perhaps two-hundred years earlier.

"Captain Castor immediately struck a deal with his crew where everyone would share in the treasure, from the lowest seaman to the captain himself and his First Mate. He did this so there would be no mutiny; he had clearly seen the greed in his men's eyes when they saw the pendant rise out of the sea. Captain Castor was convinced he would not make it to shore alive if he did not take some preemptive action.

"With each man receiving a share, the men worked with efficiency and vigor and soon salvaged the galleon's treasure. It was one of the largest Spanish treasures ever found in the Keys."

"So, how did you come to know Captain Castor?"

"The captain has worked with the Pinkertons for many years, mostly transporting our agents around the Caribbean and the Keys. He still does a job for us now and then."

"As rich as he is?" asked Merritt.

"I think he enjoys the excitement of working for the Pinkerton Agency too much to give up the little dramas we occasionally throw his way, even 'though he certainly does not need the money."

When they reached *The Crow's Nest*, Merritt and Kate were led by the maître d' to a table for four at the back of the restaurant. There a small man with weathered brown skin and white hair was in deep conversation with the woman next to him. When he saw Kate and Merritt, he stood up to greet them. He was wearing a red linen jacket over white pants and a white, open-necked shirt. "Kate!" he exclaimed, leaning forward to kiss her cheek. Captain Castor then turned to Merritt and shook his hand. "And you must be Merritt! I have looked forward to making your acquaintance." Then Captain Castor placed his hand gently on the other woman's shoulder. "And this," he said with obvious affection, "is my wife Viola."

Viola Castor was a matronly woman, bronzed by the sun with

deep wrinkles around her mouth and eyes. She was dressed in a simple blue dress which would have been unremarkable if it were not for the gold choker she wore, attached to which was an emerald the size of a fifty-cent piece. The stone was as clear as a tropical sea; Merritt was mesmerized by the play of light within the stone and found it hard to tear his eyes away from the pendant. *Tonight, I will introduce you to a man who bathes in Spanish gold and drapes his wife in pirate booty,* Kate had said.

As the women chatted with Captain Castor, Merritt glanced around the restaurant. Except for the tropical motif—bamboo chairs and potted palms—it was not much different from any fine restaurant in Columbus or Nashville: the waiters and busboys rushed around under the watchful eye of the maître d' and soft laughter and the clink of fine crystal filled the air. When the waiter came to get their order, Captain Castor turned to Merritt and asked, "Have you been to Key West before, Merritt?"

Merritt shook his head. "I have not," he answered.

"Ah. Then perhaps you will permit me to order for all of us? Our local food is a wonderful mix of Bahamian, Cuban, Spanish, and Indian influences. It can be a bit confusing to first time visitors."

"Gladly," answered Merritt, and the captain turned to the waiter: "We will start with an oyster cocktail. Then, a conch ceviche, and, for the main course, hogfish. Please ask the Chef to bake the fish with a ginger, lime and butter sauce." As the waiter turned to leave, Captain Castor added, "And bring us more water as well."

The water, as it turned out, was an act of mercy on the captain's part. The 'oyster cocktail' was a half-dozen raw oysters stirred in a glass with whiskey, Worcestershire, and hot sauce. The captain raised his glass and said, "Welcome to our guests!" Merritt and Kate smiled and raised their own glasses: "To new friends," Merritt said. They watched as Captain Castor swallowed his drink in a single draught, his Adam's apple pulsing as the raw oysters slid down his throat. Kate gave Merritt a look of resignation and took a long drink of her own cocktail. Her face turned red, and a sweat broke out on her forehead as she placed the glass back on the table. "Delicious," she croaked, as she reached for her water. Merritt drank his own with much the same effect, while Viola gave Captain Castor a dark look which said, *you can be such a child.*

After dinner, Captain Castor said goodbye to his wife and led Kate and Merritt into the bar which occupied a corner of the restaurant. Floor-to-ceiling shelves which contained liquor bottles of every size and color lined the wall behind a mahogany bar. Separation from the restaurant was created by a series of low planters filled with small palms and ferns.

Kate and Merritt ordered sherry while Captain Castor asked for rum. *Once a sailor, always a sailor*, thought Merritt. When they had been served, Kate explained to the captain why they were in Key West and talked about the death of the lawyer named Vernon. "They seem always to be just a step ahead of us," she said.

"I did not know Vernon well, but I saw him around town now and again," said the captain. "His reputation—no disrespect to the dead—was a bit sketchy. What do you think his connection to the robbery was?"

"He served as a conduit for messages to the mysterious 'A.H.,' whose location we hoped to learn from Mr. Vernon," answered Kate.

Captain Castor thought for a moment and then said, "I know of no one with the initials A.H."

"He must be here in the keys," said Merritt. "Have you heard of any suspicious group of men?"

Captain Castor laughed. "Before the War, I knew the name of every man in the Keys. But since the War ended, there has been a large influx of Bahamians, Cubans and others."

Kate looked so crestfallen that Captain Castor placed his hand on her arm and said, "But I have crews making deliveries to nearly every occupied island. Give me a day or two to ask around."

"Be careful, captain," said Kate. "The men we are after react harshly to any threat, perceived or real."

CHAPTER 15

Plans Develop

In preparing for battle I have always found that plans are useless, but planning is indispensable. —Dwight D. Eisenhower

The next morning, Kate and Merritt decided to take a walk before the heat of the day set in. It was still warm, but the ever-present humidity was made tolerable by a soft breeze. They walked arm-in-arm up and down the streets, Merritt wearing a straw hat that he had purchased the day before and Kate shaded by her pink parasol. They were a handsome couple and many heads turned to watch them as they walked by. There seemed a wonderful normalcy to it as they strolled and chatted, and Kate kept a tight hold on Merritt's arm. She knew that any time they had alone and temporarily disconnected from their deadly quest, was a gift. But if they had not been distracted, they might have noticed the man who stepped quickly into the shadows as they approached. Lieutenant Betron, dressed in civilian clothes, turned his back on Merritt and Kate and pretended to be lighting a pipe. When they had passed, he let out a sigh of relief. He recognized them from Dover and knew what their presence in Key West must mean.

Lieutenant Betron walked quickly to the wharf where he

found his sloop's crew of three napping in the shade. He kicked the nearest man awake and said, "Change of plans. Take me back to the island right now."

The man glanced around sleepily. "Where are the supplies?" he asked.

"Change of plans," Betron said again. "We need to get back to the island."

As they approached the intersection of Angela and Margaret Streets, Kate saw the entrance to the Key West Cemetery. She turned to Merritt and said, "Oh, Merritt, look! Would you mind if we walked through the cemetery? Does that seem ghoulish to you?"

Merritt smiled and shook his head. *"Let us talk of graves, of worms, and epitaphs;"* he answered. Kate smiled and finished the Shakespeare quote: *"Make dust our paper and with rainy eyes, Write sorrow on the bosom of the earth, Let's choose executors and talk of wills."* Laughing together, they walked into the small cemetery. Although Kate and Merritt noticed little change in elevation, the cemetery had been built on the highest point of the island after the original burial ground had been destroyed by a hurricane in 1846. It was truly a 'city of the dead,' with narrow lanes bordered by white-washed vaults. But the only citizens besides the deceased were the lizards and chickens which climbed on the vaults and pecked at the weeds which had sprouted everywhere. There were no trees and there was a general sense of decay, both corporal and spiritual. Merritt found the place neither welcoming nor comforting. Nonetheless, Kate enjoyed reading the monument inscriptions. They were, she told Merritt, like short novels, telling joyful stories (like couples blessed to share their love together into their nineties), poignant stories and tragic ones. On more than one occasion, Merritt saw Kate dab at her eyes as they passed the graves of infants and children, often marked by their distraught parents with statues of lambs or cherubs.

By noon, the sun was high in the sky and the temperature had begun to soar. The light breeze could no longer keep the humidity at bay or provide comfort from the heat. Kate and Merritt reluctantly made their way back to the Inn where there was a note waiting for them from Captain Castor. It asked them to join him again that evening at *The Crow's Nest*.

As Merritt and Kate walked to *The Crow's Nest* that evening, each was lost in their own thoughts, and they spoke little. Kate remembered Merritt's emotional collapse at the ambush site, and she worried what would happen to him as they resumed their mission to find the killers of his son. But Merritt's thoughts were darker, like a predator that had caught the scent of blood; the fire in his belly, temporarily tamped down by the presence of Kate and the lethargy of Key West, leapt to life. He sensed—no, he knew—that they were getting close to A.H. and his collaborators.

When they arrived at the restaurant, the Maître d' took them directly to the bar area. There they found Captain Castor sitting alone at a table in the corner, a mug of rum in front of him. Merritt tried to read the captain's expression, to sense what he had learned, but he was inscrutable. The captain rose to greet them and again kissed Kate's cheek. As he pulled away, Captain Castor said to Kate, "I did not notice that scar on your cheek before."

Kate instinctively touched her face and said, "You are not supposed to. I am usually more proficient in the application of my powder than I am tonight."

"A souvenir?" asked the captain. "It looks like a bullet graze."

"A souvenir from my first visit to the Shenandoah Valley of Virginia," she answered. When the captain tilted his head questioningly, Kate said, "A story for another time, captain."

"I look forward to hearing it. Now, can I get anyone a drink before I tell you what I learned today?"

Merritt, who was quickly running out of patience, said, "Please, captain, tell us what you have learned. Then I will pick the appropriate liquor for my degree of pleasure or disappointment."

"Very well," said Captain Castor. "As I said last night, since the War has ended, there has been a great influx of people into the Keys. Mostly Bahamians, many Cubans, but also some white men with grandiose plans for growing pineapples and such. But one group stands out, at least to my crews, if only for their lack of enterprise. They do not till, they do not harvest, and they have built nothing beyond what is necessary for their immediate survival. They give the appearance of waiting, but for what is not clear."

Kate and Merritt glanced at each other. "And where are they located?" asked Merritt.

"Little Torch Key," answered the captain. "Most of the southern part of the island is marshy, but there have been numerous small settlements on the north end over the years. But each failed for one reason or another."

"Do your crews still supply Little Torch Key?" asked Kate.

Captain Castor shook his head. "We delivered building supplies 3 or 4 months ago and vittles for a month or two after that. But they have a deep water pier and have obtained their own boat. My men tell me they see them occasionally at the wharf here in Key West."

Kate could sense the excitement building in Merritt. "And how many men are on the key?" he asked.

Captain Castor leaned back in his chair and began to calculate: "The leader is an older man with a white beard, I been told. He never seems to leave the island. Then, there are about 3 or 4 others, hard to keep count of as they come and go."

"Any hired workers?"

"Crew for the sloop, mebbe three altogether. A Bahamian cook, I believe, and an old Seminole man that does the chores. That is all I was told of."

Merritt leaned back in his chair and announced, "I will take that drink now, captain. Make it your best brandy!"

Captain Castor rose from his chair and looked at Kate: "And you, Kate?"

"Just water, please, captain," Kate answered. She did not share Merritt's obvious enthusiasm over the information that Captain Castor had just provided them. Her instincts told her that blood would soon flow, staining the sand and tinting the crystalline waters of the Keys. Kate could smell it in the air, prophetic of the damned and soon to die.

Merritt and Captain Castor toasted each other and Kate. "To justice!" said Merritt. "To justice," answered the captain. Kate smiled slightly but said nothing.

When Merritt finished his brandy, he said, "Can you provide us a boat to reconnoiter Little Torch Key, captain?"

"Of course. And I will provide you a crew as well. When would you like it available?"

Merritt looked surprised. "Why, tomorrow," he answered.

Kate held on to Merritt's arm tightly as they walked back to the Inn. He was clearly distracted and spoke little. Kate knew that finding the men was one thing but bringing them to justice was another; they were former soldiers and had already proven themselves ruthless and cruel. She doubted they could be taken alive and would extract a terrible cost from those who tried. Kate turned to Merritt and said, "Merritt, you have fulfilled your promise to find the men who killed your son. Now why do you not let the Army come and arrest them?"

Merritt's jaw dropped. "I found them, and by God, I will finish this!" he said with such forcefulness that Kate dropped his arm and took a step backwards. When Merritt saw Kate's distress, he said, "I am sorry Kate! I did not mean to snap at you." He tried to retake her arm, but Kate pulled away. "I am concerned that the Army cannot, or will not, act quickly enough and these men will again slip through our fingers," he tried to explain. Then, when

Kate still did not respond, "Let us discuss this again tomorrow. My intention is only to confirm that our prey is where we think they are and to observe the lay of the land. I promise there will be no contact."

CHAPTER 16

Aboard the 'Viola Mae'

*One will not break through to the enemy with theory.
Directness is most important, when in front of the lion's
den...—Rati Tsiteladze*

The next morning at 5:00 a.m., Merritt and Kate were at Pier 4 as Captain Castor had instructed them. There they found the sloop Viola Mae moored to the pier. She was larger than they had expected, over one-hundred feet long with a 25' beam and painted in gay colors: light-blue to the red waterline and coral-pink railings and a yellow superstructure. She was made to appear even larger than she was by a bowsprit that Merritt guessed was at least 30' long.

The *Viola Mae* normally carried a crew of six, not only to sail her but also to on- and off-load her cargo. But today there were only three, apparently enough to efficiently run the boat if no cargo was to be carried. All three wore sailors' white canvas trousers with dark cotton jackets over white shirts; two had on wide-brimmed fedoras and the third wore a top hat.

The man in the top hat stepped forward and invited Kate and Merritt to board. The gangway was a narrow plank that extended from the pier and over the gunwale and the man held the hand of Kate as she made her way across and jumped to the deck.

When Kate and Merritt were aboard, the man removed his hat and bowed formally to Kate. He was rewarded by one of Kate's bright smiles and a tip of the hat from Merritt.

"My name," the sailor said, "is John Frost, and I am skipper of this here fine boat." Pointing at each of the other sailors in turn, he continued: "The tall one there is Amos Friend and the other Ned Massey. Captain Castor has told us to deny you both nothing."

"And did Captain Castor tell you our destination today?" asked Merritt.

John Frost nodded. "Aye, he did. Little Torch Key."

"How long do you think it will take us to reach there?"

John Frost scratched at his beard. "Little Torch Key is rounds about 25 miles as a crow flies, but more like 35 for us as we must go wide around some hazards. With a fair breeze, we should be able to make ten knots easy. Safe side: mebbe three to four hours."

As the *Viola Mae* made her way out of the harbor, Kate and Merritt sat in the shade of the mainsail trying to stay out of the way as the sailors bustled about raising sails and coiling ropes. When the sails were set, John Frost took his position behind a large tiller on the aft deck that steered the boat, and his men went to busy themselves with other tasks. Kate stood up and walked unsteadily across the moving deck. When she reached the skipper, she said, "Mr. Frost, I am curious about something. I have seen so many boats since coming to Key West, of every size and purpose, yet nearly all call themselves a 'sloop.' How can that be?"

John Frost smiled at Kate. "Ah, well, missus, size and purpose got nothing to do with it. A sloop is any boat with a single mast, a headsail forward of the mast and a mainsail aft." He glanced at the compass and adjusted his course a bit. "Now," he continued, "a sloop generally has one of two sail rigs: what is called a 'Bermuda rig,' with triangular sails fore and aft, or a 'gaff-rig.' A gaff-rig means a two-part mainsail with a triangular foresail."

Kate glanced aloft at the sails on the *Viola Mae*. "A gaff-rig?" she asked. John Frost smiled at her as if she were his prize student. "Yes, Missus, we will make a sailor out of you yet."

Kate smiled back. "We shall see about that, Mr. Frost." Then, "Is one rig preferable over another?"

John Frost shrugged. "Depends. A Bermuda rig is simpler to manage, even a single crew member can do it. She also sails closer into the wind than a gaff-rig. But the gaff-rig provides more sail area and greater power, useful for freighters like the *Viola Mae*."

Kate thanked the skipper for his time and returned to her seat next to Merritt. "What were you two talking about?" he asked. Kate shrugged her shoulders and answered, "Mostly the relative merits of a gaff-rig versus a Bermuda-rig."

"Ah," Merritt said, smiling.

Kate took great, deep breaths of the fresh ocean air. She had never been to sea before, but she quickly adapted to the rhythmic movement of the boat; it was, she realized, not unlike riding a horse English style, your body moving in exaggerated concert with the horse's movements. Although she still questioned the wisdom of Merritt's desire to 'reconnoiter' Little Torch Key, she enjoyed the trip itself more than she had expected. But not so for Merritt: his complexion had taken on an unhealthy green hue, and he emptied his stomach over the lee gunwale several times.

Three hours after they left Key West, Little Torch Key rose up out of the sea in front of them. As they approached the little island from the south, they saw it was ringed with palm trees and mangrove swamps, but they saw no sign of a settlement.

Merritt turned to the Skipper. "Are you sure this is Little Torch Key, Mr. Frost?"

"Aye, Mr. Cowles. I have delivered freight here in the past. The island is 'round 2 1/2 miles long and there is a small pier at the north end."

"Then let us circle the island and take a look at it from 'stem to stern' as you sailors say."

"If your purpose is to be stealthy, Mr. Cowles, that might not be advisable. The channel on the west side of the island is shallow and most often only a few hundred yards wide. But in the channel to the east, we can stand offshore close to a half-mile. It will give you a look at the north end and should not attract attention."

"Very well," said Merritt, his disappointment obvious in his voice.

Kate placed her hand nervously on the pistol she carried in a shoulder holster. Every instinct she had was screaming at her to get far away from Little Torch Key as fast as she possibly could.

Colonel Hollingsworth sat in a small study he had made for himself. The clapboard walls were bare except for a tattered Confederate battle flag the colonel had retrieved himself from the battlefield at Shiloh. He was writing his memoirs. Colonel Hollingsworth had the remarkable ability to mentally relive episodes of his life, remembering every sight and smell; when he wrote, it was as if events were happening at that very moment. So deep was his reverie, that he was known to write day and night for 2 or more days, never stopping to eat, never sleeping. But this time he was brought back to reality by the small boy Sammy standing in the front yard yelling, "A sail, Sir colonel."

Colonel Hollingsworth leapt to his feet and ran outside. "Where? And how far out?" he asked.

"South side," Sammy answered. "She just come over the horizon."

The colonel swore under his breath and walked out onto the front porch where he rang a bell that had been hung to announce meals. It also served as a 'call to arms.' Within a few minutes, all the men had gathered in the front yard. "Sammy saw a sail approaching from the south," said the colonel. "Probably just a trader, but no need to take chances." Colonel Hollingsworth had kept them all on heightened alert since Lieutenant Betron had told him of his sighting of the mysterious man and woman in Key West. "Go to your positions," he continued, "but take no action unless you hear me ring the bell. Remember: three bells if they use the east channel and 4 for the west."

The men nodded and turned to go to their assigned positions. They were heavily armed with pistols and rifles, and each carried at least forty rounds of ammunition. They had no idea what size force might confront them, and they wanted to be ready. In a way, it was the colonel's trademark. He had once told a subordinate, "You can never be overprepared, but you sure as hell can be underprepared."

Earl Hassler and Lieutenant Betron made their way to the sloop moored to the pier on the north side of the island, which the crew called the *Pajarito*, Spanish for 'Little Bird.' Betron told the small crew that awaited them there to be ready to sail with a moment's notice. At the same time, Cyril Winebrenner made his way to a sharpshooter's nest that had been constructed on the east side of the island where the deeper, wider channel lay. But, on the colonel's insistence, a second nest had been built on the opposite side of the island to protect the west channel if need be; the key was no more than ½ mile wide at this point and Cyril could quickly move to the other side of the island if he needed to.

Colonel Hollingsworth walked around the main building and quickly climbed to the top of an observation tower he had constructed when they first came to the island. It was just slightly less high than the tops of the palm trees, but high enough that a man could see over the top of them without being exposed. He had a clear 360o view around the little island.

Colonel Hollingsworth quickly located the boat with his telescope, and he estimated she was still more than 3,000 yards out. As Sammy had said, it was approaching the island from the south at what seemed a leisurely pace. What danger she represented, if any, was yet to be determined.

Cyril stood with a pair of brass binoculars around his neck and a rifle wrapped in burlap in his hands. He nodded approvingly at the sharpshooter's nest that had been built to his specifications: brush and palms along the water had been trimmed to fully reveal the waterway in front of him, giving him nearly a 180° field of view. For protection, he had a 2' high log wall that he could hide behind and could also be used as a rest for his rifle to steady his aim.

Cyril sat down on a tree stump and carefully unwrapped his rifle. It was an English Whitworth rifle, forty-nine inches long with a Malcom telescopic sight attached to the left side of the barrel. Cyril had taken it from a dead Confederate sharpshooter and quickly became so adept at its use that he had become one of his companies most effective sharpshooters. He had even become momentarily famous for killing a Confederate general at 1,100 yards, an unheard-of feat. To commemorate the shot, Cyril had taken one of his hexagonal bullets and wore it around his neck on a rawhide lace. But what Cyril had not bothered to explain was that he had probably fired a dozen shots at the man before he finally hit him. With the cacophony of battle, the general had never heard the distinctive fluttering sound of the Whitworth's hexagonal rounds coming at him, so distinctive from the buzz of the Minié balls. If he had, the sound might have warned him of the danger he was in. Nonetheless, within eight hundred yards, Cyril rarely missed.

Cyril breathed in the odor of the gun oil as if it were a lover's perfume as he caressed the rifle's stock. The rifle was the only thing in this world that Cyril loved. He had been teased incessantly about his weight as a child and he grew up bitter, lonely and without empathy. He finally found his meaning in the War where empathy and mercy were not required for a soldier nor even necessarily desirable. He was fearless and deadly.

Like Cyril, the Whitworth rifle was the perfect killing machine. Although it was still a muzzle-loader at a time when repeating weapons were becoming popular, it was nonetheless the most accurate rifle ever made up to that time. Its effective range was 800-1,000 yards, although it could easily reach 1,500 yards. And an expert like Cyril could reload and fire it 2 to 3 times per minute.

Cyril removed a tobacco tin from his pocket and placed it on the log beside him. It contained 20 hexagonal rounds for the Whitworth rifle protected by a bed of cotton. Cyril had cast them and then weighed them each individually to insure that they weighed 530 grams, no more no less. Any variation in weight would affect the consistency of his shots. Similarly, he had weighed and re-weighed the paper cartridges of powder to insure they were all seventy grams. He placed the powder cartridges and a tin of percussion caps on the log next to the hexagonal rounds and sat back to wait for the colonel's signal, reflexively fiddling with the spent cartridge around his neck.

CHAPTER 17

The First Battle of Little Torch Key

It's better to train for a battle that never comes, than to die in one you aren't prepared for. —*Erin Hunter*

Colonel Hollingsworth watched the boat continue its approach from the south towards Little Torch Key. When she reached the point where she must decide which channel to follow, the boat was probably no more than 1,800 yards away. Colonel Hollingsworth rested his telescope on the platform railing and squinted at the boat. It was still too far away for him to make out faces, but he could distinguish the crew members and passengers individually, at least those above deck. None looked to be wearing a military uniform, but one appeared to be wearing a dress.

Colonel Hollingsworth squinted so hard through the telescope that his eye began to water. Then, when the boat began her turn into the east channel, the woman turned and stared straight at the colonel. The sensation that she was looking back at him was so strong that Colonel Hollinsworth quickly lowered the telescope. *Well,* he thought, *if you are looking for me, Miss, you have found me.* He climbed quickly down the platform's ladder and ran into the front yard and onto the front porch. There he grabbed the dinner bell's clapper and swung it hard, three times.

A flock of colorful birds, startled by the sound, rose from nearby bushes and danced across the sky.

Colonel Hollingsworth turned and casually made his way back to the observation platform. He was in no hurry. He knew that he no longer had any control over how the day's events would turn out. He could only hope that he had made the appropriate preparations. So it always was when the battle is joined.

Cyril heard the bell ring three times, and he began to hum a cheerful little tune. Momentarily, at least, he forgot about the heat and niggling insects as he loaded his rifle, careful not to spill even a single grain of gunpowder. He stood the gun against the log wall and walked to the edge of the water. He looked to the south, but the boat had not yet come into view. He sat down again behind the log wall and mentally prepared for his first shot based on information he had received from the crew of the colonel's sloop. They had told him that the actual boat channel was no more than 150 yards wide and lay around 500 yards east of his position, which meant he would be shooting between 500 and 650 yards. Based on that information, Cyril made some preliminary adjustments to the telescopic sight. Then he picked up the binoculars—they had a much greater field of vision than the telescopic sight—and scanned the channel in front of him. At something over 1,500 yards across the channel, he could see Big Pine Key shimmering in the tropical heat. But Cyril was only interested in any rippling of the surface of the water that would indicate wind, another possible deterrent to his accuracy. He saw no indications of anything more than a light breeze. Then Cyril did something that few of his companions had ever seen him do: he smiled.

When Lieutenant Betron heard the three bells, he ordered the sloop's crew of three to set sail. In no time, the mainsail and foresails were set, and they were moving down the small inlet and into the west channel. The lieutenant and Earl Hassler braced themselves against the gunwale as the sloop began to roll a bit. Each carried short-barreled Spencer repeating rifles as well as sidearms. They watched Little Torch Key slide by as they made their way to their assigned position at the south end of the island. When the interlopers had had enough of Cyril's sharp-shooting and made to escape, Lieutenant Betron and Earl would be waiting for them.

Kate could not escape the feeling that they were being watched. She strained to scan the island ahead of them but saw nothing except palm trees and palmetto bushes. She glanced over at Merritt, who was leaning against the main mast with his arms crossed. Beside him was his new Spencer carbine which he had purchased at the beginning of their trip. The rifle's brass gleamed in the sunshine. When Merritt felt Kate looking at him, he picked up his rifle and walked over to her. "I see nothing at all," he said. "Perhaps A.H. and his cronies have fled." But Kate did not think so, although she did not say so to Merritt. They stood in silence as the *Viola Mae* sailed slowly up the coast of Little Torch Key, some seven-hundred yards off their port side.

As the sloop came into view, Cyril put the binoculars down and picked up his rifle. He could now see the passengers and crew clearly through his telescopic sight. He framed Kate's face in the sight; *pretty*, he thought. Then he moved to the tall man standing next to her. With his erect posture and neatly trimmed beard, he gave the impression of being an aristocrat. Cyril hated him on sight. Then Cyril counted the crew: one man at the tiller and two others adjusting the sails and coiling lines. There could be more below deck, but he did not think so.

Cyril knew he should start with the man at the tiller, who was probably the captain of the boat, and thereby disable it. But instead, he steadied his sight on Merritt. There was plenty of time, he reckoned, to deal with the rest. The boat's movement caused the image in the sight to move just as Cyril squeezed the trigger. Cyril knew he had missed the moment the rifle fired. *Damn, Cyril*, he said to himself, *time the rise and fall of the boat.*

On board the *Viola Mae*, Kate and Merritt heard a gunshot from Little Torch Key just before something passed over their heads making a strange fluttering sound. "What was that?" asked Merritt. Kate instinctively ducked below the gunwale, trying to pull Merritt down with her when a second shot rang out. This time, it was followed by a smacking sound, like an axe handle striking a wet sack and Merritt fell to the deck. "No!" Kate screamed as she rushed to his side. He had been struck in the thigh and blood was pouring onto the deck. Kate quickly tore a piece of cloth from the hem of her dress and tied a tourniquet above the wound. She could not tell if the bone had been broken. Merritt's grimaced at the pain but remained conscious.

Kate turned to John Frost, still at the tiller, who was staring at them open-mouthed. "It is a sharpshooter, Mr. Frost. Make yourself a small target and so advise your crew."

The tiller was totally exposed on the aft deck and John Frost could only hunch over, trying to keep his head below the level of the gunwale. He had no real option to seek cover; he knew that if he left the tiller they would run aground, and all would be lost.

As the *Viola Mae* made her way northward up the little channel, the breeze changed direction slightly and the mainsail began to flap uselessly. Amos Friend jumped up from his hiding place and pulled the sail taught. For a few moments, he was hidden from Little Torch Key by the mainsail, but when he tried to return to cover, the sharpshooter found him. His body spun around at the impact of the bullet, and he fell overboard. John Frost let out a cry of dismay, but he dared not stop to try and rescue his friend and crew mate.

Kate held Merritt's hand and shouted at the skipper, "You must get us out of here, Mr. Frost. We are sitting ducks."

"Aye, Missus," John Frost said, as he tried to calm his mind. He knew that the channel they were in was less than two-hundred yards wide and he had no idea exactly what their true position was. If they were too close to the edge of the channel, they might run aground attempting to make a turn. He tried not to think about what that would mean for them. But what way should he make the turn, port or starboard? "Prepare to come about!" he yelled, as he pushed the tiller hard to starboard. He hoped that God had led him to make the right choice. *Holy Mary, Mother of God, pray for us sinners, now and at the hour of our death.*

Kate watched as the boom swung over her head. There was a sickening moment when the mainsail lost the wind and the boat lost most of its forward momentum, almost coming to a stop. But then the sail filled with a loud crack and the *Viola Mae* once again surged forward.

Cyril had no clear targets, so he contented himself with harassing the boat. He picked out various objects on the boat's superstructure and plinked at them like a boy shooting at bottles in a dump. On the *Viola Mae*, each shot from shore raised their anxiety more as they awaited each round to strike its target.

When the *Viola Mae* finally disappeared around the south end of the island, Cyril picked up his rifle and equipment and casually walked back to the compound. He had done his part and now it was up to Lieutenant Betron and Earl Hassler to finish them off.

Everyone aboard the *Viola Mae* breathed a sigh of relief when the relentless sniping finally stopped. But their relief was short-lived when they saw a small sloop come around the tip of the island and turn in their direction. *Friend or foe?* Kate wondered. She got her answer when two men on the approaching sloop opened fire with a barrage of shots that could only have come from repeating rifles. The rounds fell short but had made their intentions clear. "Can we outrun them, Mr. Frost?"

John Frost shook his head. "Not likely, Missus. She appears half the size and weight of the *Viola Mae*."

The second boat was around seven-hundred yards away and closing rapidly when a voice, amplified by a megaphone, said, "Heave to and you will come to no harm."

Kate picked up Merritt's rifle, aimed at a spot some twenty feet above the other sloop and fired. She came surprisingly close to the boat. "Eloquent answer," said Merritt approvingly, surprising Kate.

"Why thank you, Mr. Cowles. How is your wound?"

"Hurts like hell."

"Can you fire a weapon?"

Merritt nodded and pulled himself into a sitting position, his shoulder against the gunwale. Kate handed Merritt his rifle and checked the load in her pistol. Then she walked over to John Frost at the tiller. While Kate and Merritt had been talking, the skipper had turned the boat to flee from the other sloop. But when Kate looked back, it was clear they were losing ground quickly, and she expected another barrage of gun fire at any moment. "Now, Mr. Frost," she said, "here is what we are going to do. I want you to turn around and run straight at that other sloop. Whatever way she turns, you turn with her. I want you to keep our bowsprit aimed directly at hers."

John Frost stared at Kate wide-eyed. "But Missus..."

Kate held up her hand to interrupt. "If we allow the other sloop to pass us broadside, we will all die. Do you understand, John?" The skipper nodded and took a deep breath. "Prepare to turn about!" he yelled. Kate returned to stand by Merritt while Ned Massey, the remaining crew member, jumped up to adjust the lines and sails. The *Viola Mae* answered the tiller smartly and turned to face their enemies. As her sails refilled, she surged forward.

Aboard the *Pajarito*, Earl Hassler turned to Lieutenant Betron and asked, "What the hell are they doing?"

"Committing suicide, I reckon," answered the lieutenant. Betron turned towards the man on the tiller and ordered, "Pass on her port or starboard side, I do not care which." The lieutenant turned again to Hassler. "One broadside and we will finish her."

The distance between the boats steadily decreased, from 700 to 600 to 500 yards. But no matter which way the *Pajarito* turned, the *Viola Mae* obstinately remained dead ahead. The crewman on the tiller told Lieutenant Betron that they should break off the pursuit and try again from another direction. But Betron's blood was up, and he wanted nothing more than to end this here and now. At a distance of 400 yards, he and Hassler again fired a volley at the *Viola Mae*. The rounds raked the deck and John Frost was nearly blinded by a splinter from a near miss, but he nonetheless held tightly to the tiller. Per Kate's instructions, he constantly adjusted their course to keep his bowsprit aimed at the very heart of the pursuer.

At three-hundred yards and again at 200, the lieutenant and Hassler raked the decks of the *Viola Mae* with gunfire. They chose no specific target because hitting a moving target from a moving platform was problematic at best. But after the last volley, for the first time, Kate stood up from behind the gunwale and emptied her pistol at the fast-approaching sloop. At the same time, Merritt emptied his rifle's magazine. Both Hassler and the lieutenant jumped for cover after a lucky shot scored the top of a hatch cover and wounded one of the crewmen who hid behind it.

Kate and Merritt rushed to reload as the two boats grew ever nearer. When Lieutenant Betron finally realized that the *Viola Mae* meant to ram them, he screamed at the man on the tiller, "Turn! Turn!"

The *Pajarito* had only made it halfway through her turn when the *Viola Mae* struck her amidships and rolled her on her side. Were it not for her centerboard, the *Viola Mae* would have completely passed over the smaller boat; as it was, she hung up halfway across and came to a grinding stop. The *Pajarito's* crew were thrown in the water and Betron and Hassler tumbled down the canted deck and into a tangle of ropes and sails and broken boards.

Kate had been violently thrown to the deck of the *Viola Mae* by the impact of the collision and it took her a moment to regain her senses while Merritt motioned to John Frost, who had never let go of the tiller even during the crash, to help him to his feet. Together, the three of them walked and hobbled to the gunwale and stared at the wreckage below.

Earl Hassler lay dead, impaled on a broken board. But Lieutenant Betron appeared unhurt and was crawling through the wreckage looking for his rifle. When he finally found it, he picked it up and only then glanced up to see two men and a woman looking down at him from the deck of the *Viola Mae*. The man held a carbine and the woman a Colt Army revolver. Both weapons were pointed at the lieutenant's heart. Lieutenant Betron sighed and carefully lowered his rifle to the deck.

"You are Lieutenant Betron," said Merritt. "We saw you in Dover."

Lieutenant Betron bowed slightly and smiled at Kate. "And I you, although I do not know your names. At least not your real names."

"I am Merritt Cowles, and this is Mrs. Kate Warne, a Pinkerton detective. This gentleman," he said, indicating John Snow, "is the skipper of this once fine vessel."

Lieutenant Betron glanced ruefully at the wreckage of the *Pajarito* around him. Then, "And what is it you want so badly from me?"

"You do not recognize my name?" Merritt asked.

"I cannot say as I do."

"My son, Allen Cowles, was a guard on the payroll train you robbed. You murdered him."

Lieutenant Betron inched closer to his rifle. "Ah, I see." The lieutenant scratched at his beard, "Now I remember. He was the one who cried for his mother." The lieutenant shook his head sadly, "A pitiful sight, that, what with the tears and snot running down his face, begging for his life."

The muscles worked in Merritt's jaw and his finger tightened on the trigger of his rifle. Kate sensed he was about to fire and yelled, "No, Merritt, no!"

Merritt was so startled by Kate's outcry that he momentarily took his eyes off Lieutenant Betron to look at her. It was then that the lieutenant dove for his rifle and raised it to fire at Kate and Merritt. But Kate was not caught by surprise. She fired three quick shots from her revolver, one of which found Lieutenant Betron's chest. Then she fired three more shots into him even when he had slumped to the ruined deck.

Exhausted by the loss of blood, Merritt slid to the deck. Kate put her arms around him and held him while he went in and out of consciousness.

CHAPTER 18

Back in Key West

That arrogance of youth and that kind of ignorant confidence can get you through a whole lot of things, and then life does its stuff, and you get smashed around and beaten up...--Robyn Davidson

John Frost and Ned Massey managed to separate the Viola Mae from the remains of the Pajarito using pulleys and brute strength. Then, John Frost conducted a quick inspection of the Viola Mae and found that several planks below water level had buckled and were leaking. Ned and he braced what they could and applied some pitch that they carried aboard. The leaks did not stop, but they did slow.

"How does it look, John?" Kate asked.

"She will float, Missus, at least long enough to get us back to Key West."

John Frost sailed the boat in a wide circle around the wreckage of the *Pajarito* hoping to find her missing crew members but found nothing. Either they had swum to a nearby island or had drowned.

The trip back to Key West was slow and arduous. Once quick

and responsive, the wounded *Viola Mae* labored through the swells and seemed to fight every change of rudder and sail. The sun was just beginning to set when they finally passed Fort Taylor and made their way into the harbor.

The *Viola Mae* had been spotted as she neared the island and word was sent to Captain Castor, who was standing on the pier when they arrived. He watched as John Frost and Ned Massey helped Merritt down the gangplank and then placed him in a wagon. Merritt was pale, barely conscious and bleeding from his leg while John Frost had a deep gash on his cheek from the wood splinter. But it was Kate who most shocked the captain; her hair was askew, and her dress tattered and soaked with blood. Her eyes were wide and unblinking.

Captain Castor rushed up to Kate. "Good Lord, Kate, are you hurt?"

Kate looked down at herself as if she had not before been aware of the blood. "No, captain, this is not my blood. It is poor Merritt's." She suddenly looked around desperately, "Oh, where is Merritt?"

Captain Caster placed his arm around Kate's shoulders. "My men have already taken him to my home where a doctor will be waiting to see him. You both will be staying with me until Merritt heals."

Kate suddenly started to sag against the captain. Rather than wait for another wagon to be found, he signaled to one of his men to help him walk her to his house. When they arrived, Viola took Kate to a guest bedroom and helped her undress. Then she helped her wash and took her clothes to be burned. By the time Viola returned to Kate's room, she had fallen into a deep sleep.

The next morning, Kate and Captain Castor sat sipping fresh lemonade on a shaded patio off the main floor of his house. Kate was wearing some of Viola's clothes while she awaited her own belongings to be retrieved from *The Fleming Inn*. Merritt was still asleep. "What happened, Kate?"

Kate shrugged her shoulders. "They were waiting for us, captain."

"But how can that be?"

"I do not know. They must have their spies. The question is, what do we do next?"

"I do not believe there is any real question about it: you must call in the Army."

Kate smiled. "Merritt will want to finish this himself."

"Then you must convince him to do otherwise. It will take an army to drive those men from Little Torch Key. We have already lost poor Amos Friend and almost lost Merritt and you never got within five-hundred yards of the shore."

Kate sighed deeply. "I am terribly sorry about Mr. Friend. And your boat, captain."

Captain Castor made a dismissive gesture. "The boat can be repaired," he said, "but I do not want to lose any more men."

"I promise you we will take no more of your men into harm's way. But I do want to talk to you about Mr. Frost."

"John?"

Kate nodded. "I believe, captain, that Mr. Frost is one of the bravest men I have ever known. We were under nearly constant fire, yet he never left the tiller for even an instant. If he had, we would surely have run aground, and all been killed."

"John is a good man. Thank you for telling me this, Kate." Captain Castor thought for a moment: "Perhaps it is time he was given greater responsibility and a larger command."

Merritt sat up straight in the bed. "The Army? Never! I will finish this myself or die trying." Kate was forever in awe of the male ego which can rarely be dissuaded by facts or common sense. So, she took a different tack: "I would never expect less, Merritt." Kate sat down on the bed next to him and took his hand. "But the doctor said you will be on crutches for several more weeks, at least. What if they escape? They have enough money to hide anywhere in the world."

Merritt grunted. "Perhaps you are right," he said. "But I do not trust the Army to act swiftly. I will contact Johnson tomorrow to speed the Army's response."

Kate raised her eyebrows. "*President* Johnson?" she asked.

Merritt shrugged. "I have been a staunch supporter of the Grand Old Party since Lincoln's candidacy. By that, I mean 'donor.' I am confident he will grant me a favor."

For the next several days, telegrams flew between Merritt and Washington and back again. It was soon agreed that the Army would send a company of 60 men to Key West to arrest anyone and everyone at Little Torch Key to face Federal charges of robbery and capital murder.

A week later—lightning fast for a peacetime Army—the promised men arrived by ship from Newport Barracks in North Carolina. Merritt, leaning heavily on a wooden crutch, stood with Kate watching as the men arrived at the main pier. Merritt had been advised by Washington that their commander was a captain named Lyle J. Cox, Jr. Merritt also saw two second lieutenants and several non-coms among the men.

The physical appearance of the men did not instill great confidence in either Merritt or Kate. The sea journey had clearly not agreed with them, and they nearly tumbled over each other in a rush to escape the ship. The non-coms could be heard yelling and cursing at them in an unsuccessful attempt to restore order.

The men were very young, and they did not appear old enough to have fought in the War; only the non-coms walked with the swagger of well-trained and experienced veterans. The two second lieutenants stood to the side and generally tried to stay out of the non-coms' way. Neither of the officers had beards and Merritt wondered if they even shaved yet.

The men slowly stopped pushing and shoving each other and

allowed the non-coms to form them into lines, although some individuals would occasionally break ranks and rush to the edge of the pier to empty their still-heaving bellies. They would then sheepishly rejoin the lines as their comrades shouted comments questioning both their manhood and their grit. Merritt and Kate overheard more than one man say, "I did not join the army to be no dang sailor."

All suddenly became quiet as Captain Cox walked down the gangplank and onto the pier. The men came to attention and the non-coms saluted. Captain Cox returned the men's salutes with a casual flick of his fingers and generally ignored the young officers who followed along behind him like two ducklings after their mother. He was resplendent in his Army uniform, a dark-blue sack coat with a captain's epaulettes which he wore over sky-blue trousers with dark blue piping. Having been in the military himself, Merritt recognized the piping as indicative of the infantry branch. On his head, the captain wore an untrimmed slouch hat.

When Captain Cox spotted Merritt and Kate standing off to the side of the pier, he dismissed his men and made his way over to them. As the captain approached, Merritt noticed that his eyes never left Kate. The captain swept off his slouch hat and bowed to Kate. "I am Captain Cox," he said

Up close, the captain's features were so remarkable that Kate was momentarily speechless. Captain Cox had bright ginger hair and a short blond beard, both of which served to frame the most beautiful eyes she had ever seen; they were the same shade of translucent-blue as the water that surrounded the Keys and they caught and held the light like a finely cut gemstone. Her mind went instantly to a Shakespeare Sonnet: *If I could write the beauty of your eyes, And in fresh numbers number all your graces, The age to come would say, 'This poet lies; Such heavenly touches ne'er touch'd earthly faces.'*

Kate blushed at her reaction to the captain. She lowered her eyes as she extended her hand and introduced herself and Merritt.

Merritt sensed Kate's visceral response to the dashing captain and perhaps squeezed a bit harder than he should have as they shook hands. Captain Cox gave him a knowing smile, which infuriated Merritt. Kate stepped in: "Captain, we would like to share with you what we have learned about the mysterious A.H. and his band of thugs on Little Torch Key. Are you able to join us for dinner this evening?"

Captain Cox smiled. "I would be delighted," he said.

"There is a restaurant called *The Crow's Nest* not too far from here. It is owned by a friend of ours and it is quite private. Say 7:00 p.m.?"

"7:00 p.m. it is. Now I must go see to my men." The captain tipped his hat to Kate and nodded at Merritt. "Until this evening."

As Captain Cox walked away, Merritt said softly, "I do not like that man."

"For goodness' sake why?" Kate asked. "You just met him."

Merritt wrestled with the question for a moment and then just blurted out, "I do not care for the way he looked at you."

Kate's eyes widened and then she smiled. "Why Mr. Cowles, I do believe you are jealous!"

"Nonsense!"

Kate took Merritt's hand. "You have no need to be jealous of any man, Merritt. I love only you."

When Merritt did not respond right away, tears sprang from Kate's eyes. "Oh, I am sorry, Merritt, I should never have said that! Please, let us forget I ever said anything."

"No," said Merritt, "I shall never forget it." He placed his hands on both sides of her face and kissed her tears away. "I am such a coward," he said. "I think I have loved you from the day we first met and yet I said nothing. What if you had lost patience with me and I had lost you?"

Kate touched Merritt's face with her fingers. "You will never lose me, Merritt."

Merritt, Kate, Captain Cox, and Captain Castor sat at a table in the rear of the bar at *The Crow's Nest* restaurant. They had spent their dinner in the restaurant in casual conversation, carefully avoiding the topic of Little Torch Key and its inhabitants. Captain Cox sensed that something had changed between Kate and Merritt; there were surreptitious glances between them, and Merritt had greeted Captain Cox with a warmth clearly missing from their first meeting.

When Merritt and Kate had finished telling Captain Cox of their ill-fated trip to Little Torch Key, the captain sat back in his chair with a thoughtful expression on his face. "Yet, you say there were no more than 4 or 5 men?"

"Plus three or 4 others who crewed the sloop and maintained the compound. But we do not believe they were combatants," answered Kate.

Captain Cox shook his head. "I do not know that a half-dozen men warrant a full company of soldiers."

"I would warn you not to underestimate these men, captain," said Merritt. "We have every reason to believe they are professional soldiers..."

Captain Cox interrupted with a wave of his hand. "Fear not, Mr. Cowles, we will bring this mighty band of miscreants to their knees." Then he turned to Captain Castor. "I believe we will need no more than two boats as I will take no more than 20 men. And, as we discussed earlier, the boats will be crewed solely by volunteers who will be paid by the Government." With that, Captain Cox rose and bowed to Kate. After shaking Merritt's and Captain Castor's hands, he turned and walked out of the bar.

"I do not like that man," said Captain Castor.

CHAPTER 19

The Armada of Lyle J. Cox, Jr.,

Captain, U.S. Army

Arrogance on the part of the meritorious is even more offensive to us than the arrogance of those without merit: for merit itself is offensive. — *Friedrich Nietzsche*

I t took another day for Captain Cox to raise a volunteer crew for his mission to Little Torch Key. By this time, everyone in Key West had heard about the debacle on the Viola Mae. But the proffered wages were good and on the third day after his arrival, Captain Cox had his crews. He and his twenty men left at dawn and sailed past Fort Taylor, where the men on the ramparts snapped sharp salutes at the passing boats. The breeze stiffened, and the swells grew in size as the two sloops turned northwards. The decks rose and fell and rocked from side to side; everything seemed always to be moving and twisting as if the boats themselves had become living things. Under their breath, Captain Cox's men cursed him, the boats and whatever had compelled them to join the Army in the first place.

With events out of their control, Kate and Merritt spent the day sitting in the shade on Captain Castor's patio. They had moved their chairs next to each other where they could maintain physical contact, holding hands or touching each other to emphasize a conversation point. Merritt, who had placed his injured leg on a stool in front of him, was the center of attention from both Kate and Viola. He wanted for nothing, from a cushion for his injured leg to an endless supply of freshly squeezed lemonade with ice from the local icehouse. *Not a bad life*, he thought, as he leaned back in his chair, smiling.

As if reading his mind, Kate said, "Do not become too used to this, Mr. Cowles."

Merritt smiled at Kate. "Am I to blame because I am spoiled merely by being in your presence?" he asked, as he reached for her hand.

Kate touched his face. "You have a silver tongue, Mr. Cowles. Sometimes I think you more lawyer than banker."

Merritt pretended to shudder. "You cut me to the quick, Mrs. Warne!"

Merritt and Kate spent the rest of the afternoon telling each other about their childhoods and their lives before they met. Viola would check in on them periodically, but she left them mostly alone as it was clear they delighted in their time together; but Viola also sensed a desperation in the way they clung to each other. It was if they both worried that someone or some event would come tear them apart at any moment.

When Merritt began telling Kate about his military experience, it surprised her. "You really went to West Point?" she asked.

"I did," he answered. "Class of '46."

"Goodness!" Then, "1846... Was that not the beginning of the Mexican-American War?"

"It was. My class graduated just weeks after the War began. Nearly all of us—shavetails all—went to fight in Mexico."

"'Shavetails,'" repeated Kate. "That is an odd word."

Merritt laughed. "It is a rather derogatory term for newly minted second lieutenants. Their minds are stuffed with military tactics and history, yet they have never heard the angry buzz of Minié balls nor led men into combat." Merritt shrugged his shoulders. "I guess you could call war their post-graduate education."

"But you chose not to make the military your career?"

"It was not a life for me. West Point had been my Daddy's dream, really. But there were men in my class who seemed born to serve and lead: George McClellan, Thomas 'Stonewall' Jackson and even George Pickett, the class 'goat.'" Merritt anticipated Kate's question and added, "The class 'goat' is the Cadet with the lowest grades."

"What were they like as young men? McClellan, Jackson and Pickett, I mean."

Merritt gazed up at the clear blue sky thoughtfully. "Well, McClellan and Picket were pretty regular young men, more interested in women and drink than Historiography, especially Georgie Pickett. But Jackson, he was a surly character with cold eyes and a hot temper. He would as soon fight you as talk to you. He did not have many friends, as I remember."

By dark, the two sloops had still not returned to Key West. Captain Castor paced nervously on the pier for two more hours and finally returned home. Kate and Viola rushed to greet him when they heard the front door open. "Any sign of them?" Viola asked.

Captain Castor shook his head as he sat down heavily in an armchair. He asked Viola to fetch him a bottle of brandy. Then he drank the first glass in a single draught and sipped at a second. "I have men watching for their return, but no one has seen anything so far." He reached for Viola's hand and said, "I fear for their safety."

A little past 4:00 a.m., the Castor household was awakened by a pounding at the front door. Captain Castor, still dressed as he was the night before, rushed to open the door. One of his crewmen stood there nervously crushing his hat in his hands. "I am sorry to awaken you, Cap'n," he said, "but the sloops have been spotted passing Fort Taylor."

Captain Castor thanked the sailor and was about to close the door, but the man did not leave. "There is more?" asked the captain.

"Aye. They fired distress flares, Cap'n."

Captain Castor's heart sank; he knew that the flares meant there were wounded aboard. He thanked the sailor again and turned to Merritt, Kate and Viola who had also been awakened and had come up behind him. "Thank God the boats have returned but they appear to be carrying wounded men. Viola, please go to your friends and gather medical supplies. I will meet you at the pier."

Merritt placed his hand on Captain Castor's shoulder and said, "Do not let us delay you, Captain. You go on ahead. Kate and I will follow as quickly as these crutches will allow."

By the time Kate and Merritt reached the pier, the two sloops were being offloaded. They saw six soldiers sitting or lying on the pier while Viola and her friends tended to their wounds; some were unmoving while others moaned in pain. Two city doctors soon joined the ladies in their ministrations to the wounded.

Merritt saw one of the two second lieutenants standing off to the side of the wounded. As Merritt and Kate approached him, they could see blood running down his cheek. Merritt asked, "Where are the rest of your men, lieutenant?"

At first, the young officer appeared not to hear. Then he turned blankly toward Merritt and asked, "What?"

"Your men, lieutenant. Your captain and the other troops."

First understanding and then tears filled his eyes. "Dead," he said. "All dead."

Kate cleaned a deep cut on the lieutenant's forehead. When she was satisfied, she covered it with a bandage. "Better, I think. Do you suffer from any dizziness, lieutenant?"

"No, Ma'am."

"That is good." Kate glanced at Merritt as she got up to carry the bloody cotton swabs and washcloths to Captain Castor's kitchen for disposal. "I shall bring some brandy for all of us when I return."

The lieutenant looked down at his trembling hands and gave out a deep sigh. Then he turned to Merritt: "I did not know what to do. They did not train us for this."

Merritt nodded sympathetically. "There are some things for which you cannot be trained. Now, lieutenant..."

"Hendrickson, Sir. Thomas Hendrickson."

"Ah. Lieutenant Hendrickson. Do you know who the lady and I are?"

Lieutenant Hendrickson nodded. "Captain Cox said you were Pinkerton Detectives here to capture some robbers."

"Mrs. Warne is the Pinkerton. I am not. My son was killed by these men, and I am here to see they are brought to justice."

The lieutenant was about to express his sympathy to Merritt when Kate walked back in the room carrying a tray with a bottle of brandy and three glasses. When she handed a full glass to the lieutenant, his hands were shaking so badly that brandy spilled over the rim of the glass. Kate placed her hands over Lieutenant Hendrickson's and calmed the shaking, then helped him guide the glass to his mouth. After a long sip, he smiled gratefully at Kate. "Do you feel well enough to tell us what happened, lieutenant?" she asked him.

"Yes, Ma'am." The lieutenant took a deep breath. "It was savage, uncivilized. I had never even read of such things. I told Captain Cox..."

Kate held up a hand to interrupt him. "Please start at the beginning, lieutenant. Anything we can learn may be helpful."

"Yes, Ma'am." Lieutenant Hendrickson took another sip of brandy and started over...

CHAPTER 20

Lieutenant Hendrickson's Story:

The Second Battle of Little
Torch Key

...if God does not exist and there is no immortality, then all the evil acts of men go unpunished, and all the sacrifices of good men go unrewarded. –William Lane Craig

L ieutenant Hendrickson said, "Captain Cox divided us into two platoons of ten men each. Second Lieutenant Gomez-Lutino oversaw the 1st platoon and I the 2nd. We each had a single non-com assigned to our platoon.

"At dawn, we boarded the two sloops that awaited us, one platoon in each. Captain Cox rode with the 1st platoon. No sooner had we passed Fort Taylor than the wind and waves began to rise. The men, still not completely recovered from their sea voyage from Norfolk to Key West, took ill almost immediately. One man would vomit, and then the next, and it soon seemed like the whole platoon was hanging over the edge of the boat.

"The only upside to the weather was that we made good time and were approaching Little Torch Key a bit more than 2 hours later. Whatever concerns we had for what awaited us, we all would have gladly slid down a hole into Hell before spending another 10 minutes on the boat.

"Captain Cox had told us to be prepared for sharpshooter fire, but none came as we approached the single landing spot on the island. We stood offshore at about three-hundred yards while Captain Cox studied the island through his binoculars. There was no resistance of any kind and Captain Cox signaled us that he saw no sign of any inhabitants.

"I felt that the men we sought must surely have fled. After all, how I could believe that 4 or 5 men would try to resist 2 platoons of armed soldiers? Perhaps that led me to let down my guard. Or perhaps I was just cocky. This was to be my first test under fire.

"We grounded the boats one-by-one and unloaded the men. We did not disperse the men but let them stand in a gaggle as the boats returned to sea to await us offshore. I watched as Captain Cox stood exposed and unconcerned at the entrance to a path that led inland.

"Captain Cox called for double file and began to march us inland when our non-com—Sergeant Foley—rushed up to Captain Cox and begged the captain to let him lead a small group of men to scout the path ahead of us. But Captain Cox dismissed Sergeant Foley with a shake of his head. 'Let us just get this over with,' the captain said."

Lieutenant Hendrickson took another sip of brandy. "If the captain had listened to the sergeant, things might have been different. But he did not."

The lieutenant sighed and then continued his story: "So we walked up the path, barely wider than two men shoulder-to-shoulder, as if we were drilling on a parade ground.

"Mebbe one-hundred yards from the beach, the path took a sharp turn towards a small cluster of buildings at the center of the island. The captain and the rest of the 1st platoon were out of sight around the bend when the first volley of shots rang out. Although I did not see it, I reckon this was when Captain Cox was killed.

"Pandemonium ensued. Our non-com was screaming to seek cover while rounds began to snap over our heads. More men fell and their screams added to our growing panic. Judging by the rate of fire, it was clear the men we were after had repeating rifles; but how many men we were facing was unclear."

Lieutenant Hendrickson stopped and asked Kate for another brandy. But his whole body, not just his hands, had begun to shake and he could not even hold the glass. "Would you like to take a few minutes before we continue?" Kate asked.

Lieutenant Hendrickson shook his head. "No, no. Let me finish this. If I do so, perhaps it will be less inclined to haunt my sleep, although I hold little hope of that."

The lieutenant leaned back in his chair and closed his eyes. "There was no protection on the path, so we all threw ourselves into the trees and shrubbery on both sides. That is when the real horror began; the man in front of me had not taken three steps into the brush before he fell into a concealed hole. The hole had partially filled up with water, but there was a sharpened stake just below the surface upon which he impaled his leg.

"The man's screams attracted the attention of our adversaries because a greater number of bullets began to tear through the bushes and trees above our heads. God forgive me, but I cursed the man for screaming. I wanted to help him, but every time I tried to reach him, I would begin to slide down the sides of the hole and I feared what awaited me there. I watched helplessly as the water in the pit took on a darker and darker tint of crimson as the man slowly bled to death. I finally just crawled away, the man's screams growing fainter and finally stopping."

"Good Lord," said Kate. "Who ever heard of such a horrible thing?" She walked over to Lieutenant Hendrickson and placed her hand on his shoulder to comfort him. He was shaking violently, and tears were streaming down his face.

"It is called a 'trou de loup'," Merritt answered. "We studied them at the Point. They are effective and easy to build and have been in use for centuries."

Kate sighed deeply. She had seen enough of the War to know that honor was anathema to warfare; only the naive believed otherwise. "Merritt," she said, "I see no wisdom in questioning

Lieutenant Hendrickson tonight. Please take him to his room so that he may rest. We will talk again in the morning."

In the morning, Lieutenant Hendrickson was more in control of his emotions, but he was pale and hollow-eyed. It was apparent that he had not slept well if at all. When they were seated once again in Captain Castor's living room, the lieutenant turned to Kate and said, "Ma'am, I apologize for my behavior last night. I am afraid I humiliated myself and embarrassed you."

Kate frowned at the lieutenant and shook her head. "Why is it that you men always equate emotions with weakness? When will you realize that emotions are what makes us human? To survive inhumane circumstances and yet retain your humanity is to be commended, lieutenant."

The lieutenant looked unconvinced but thanked Kate for her kind words. He took a deep breath and continued his story from the night before: "There were, as you called them, Sir, *'trous de loup'* on both sides of the path. How many I do not know, but there were enough that it slowed our progress through the bush and distracted us. And there were more than just the pits; dozens of bamboo shoots had been bent in half and bound with hidden trip wires. If you stepped on the wires, the bamboo would unbend with frightening force. That is the source of my head-wound. Not lethal, but again, distracting.

"At some point, the enemy had concentrated its position where the path curved. It gave them a clear line of fire all the way to the water. We found ourselves caught between the infernal traps in the bush and certain death on the path.

"I gave orders to my men to make their way to the beach. I dismayed of seeing Captain Cox and the 1st platoon again. I believed that if they were still a functioning fighting force, they would be putting some pressure on the enemy's flank at the curve in the path. But I heard no return fire except for our own and suspected the worse.

"When I reached the landing site, I signaled for the boats to come in and pick us up. At first, they sailed straight to us, and that put them under the gun of our enemies up the path. But when bullets began landing in and around the boats, they turned and sailed down the coast; then they sailed back to us, keeping behind the cover of the bushes and palm trees that grew at the water's edge.

"Only seven of us—all members of the 2nd platoon—made it back to the boat and all of us were wounded to one degree or another. Even so, I had two of my men stand on either side of the path to warn us if the enemy chose to attack us while I waited for any other survivors to appear.

"For whatever reason, the enemy did not attack us at the shoreline. Perhaps they thought we might have reinforcements. I was uncertain what to do. What if Captain Cox and any of his men were still alive? Seeing my quandary, Sergeant Foley volunteered to go back ashore and see if he could locate the captain and his men.

"Sergeant Foley had been a scout during the War and he managed to approach the buildings at the center of the island without being seen. When he returned to the boat, he reported seeing only two men, one with a white beard and the other one tall and obese. He said there was no sign of Captain Cox or any of his men. It seems that they had all been killed at the beginning of the ambush." Lieutenant Hendrickson hesitated, then said, "There is one more thing. Sergeant Foley was close enough to overhear some of the conversation between the two men. He believes that the large man called the other man 'colonel.' I do not know if that is significant to you. At any rate, by the time Sergeant Foley returned to the boat, the sun was already beginning to set. I believe the boat crews would have preferred to wait until daylight to make the hazardous trip back to Key West, but men were dying from lack of medical care. And, truth be told, we were all of us, to a man, anxious to escape that cursed island."

After Lieutenant Hendrickson had left to return to the remains of his outfit, Kate and Merritt once again sat on Captain

Castor's patio. This time there was no lemonade, and the mood was somber. Kate looked at Merritt. "Is it possible that only 2 men were responsible for the rout of Captain Cox and his men?"

Merritt shook his head uncertainly. "I do not know. It does not seem probable. But remember that it was only 6 or 7 men that defeated the eleven military escorts with the payroll wagon train. The advent of the repeating rifle has changed how military odds are calculated; one man with a carbine is the equivalent of seven men with muskets."

"And," added Kate, "the planning of the island defense. We cannot minimize its effectiveness."

Merritt nodded in agreement. "That seems to be the signature of 'A.H.' It would serve us well not to underestimate him."

"Speaking of A.H.," Kate said, "I will send a telegram to Chicago tomorrow to see if Mr. Pinkerton can identify any colonels with those initials that served anywhere around Fort Donelson or Fort Henry. There must be some connection."

Colonel Hollingsworth sat on the front porch of his cottage and surveyed the aftermath of the fight. The Army dead lay where they fell, their bodies just beginning to swell in the tropical heat. He felt no regrets nor any special sense of pride. He had been handed a situation and he had handled it. After a short while, he got up and called for the boy Sammy. He told him to gather the boat crew and Cyril and commence digging a mass grave. The smell of decomposition was already beginning to mask the aroma of the tropical flowers that abounded around the compound, and that offended the colonel's sensibilities.

CHAPTER 21

Cowles' Army

And if you don't believe the sun will rise, stand alone and greet the coming night in the last remaining light. –Chris Cornell

After a week of convalescing, Merritt and Kate spent the rest of the day moving their belongings back to The Fleming Inn. Merritt's mobility had improved enough that he was able to care for himself and he felt no need to impose further on Captain Castor and his wife Viola. As they left Captain Castor's house, they thanked Viola profusely and shared hugs and kisses. "The captain will be sorry he missed you," said Viola. "He was short-handed and left early this morning to help with a cargo delivery to Big Coppitt Key."

"Do you know when he will return?" asked Merritt.

"I do not believe that Big Coppitt is very far from here," she answered. "And the captain did not indicate that he expected to be back too late today."

"Then please extend to him our gratitude, Viola," said Kate.

"And," added Merritt, "please tell him that Kate and I will be dining at *The Crow's Nest* tonight. If he is available, we would love to buy him a drink. And we have much to tell him."

Viola laughed. "Then I think you can count on him being there. He would swim back from Big Coppitt for a free drink!"

After dinner, Kate and Merritt took their drinks and moved into the bar. It was no more than 10 minutes later that Captain Castor arrived. He signaled the bartender for rum and rushed over to their table. He kissed Kate's hand and said, "I am so sorry to have missed you today." After shaking Merritt's hand, he sat down and said, "It is a sad state of affairs when a boat owner must offload his own cargo." He drained the mug of rum the bartender had placed in front of him and signaled for another. "There seems to be no work ethic among young people anymore. Two of my crew simply did not show up. Left me high and dry, so to speak. Ah, but forgive me, I know I rant like an old man sometimes. I assume we have more important things to talk about?"

"Some news," answered Kate. "There have been some new developments." She opened her purse and pulled out a folded telegram she had received in response to her own that afternoon. The captain glanced at it and handed it back. "Sorry, Kate, I do not have my spectacles with me."

Kate looked around and lowered her voice, "It is from Mr. Pinkerton. He believes the 'A.H.' we are seeking is Colonel Augustine Hollingsworth, one of the heroes of Shiloh, but drummed out of service no more than 6 months later."

"Goodness!" exclaimed Captain Castor. "Did Mr. Pinkerton give a reason for his dismissal?"

"Yes," said Kate, glancing at Merritt. "He was court-martialed and convicted of killing an unarmed prisoner."

"What I do not understand," said Merritt, "is why he is not in prison."

Kate shook her head. "I do not know. Perhaps it was too much of an embarrassment for the Army to imprison a full colonel and a war hero at that."

The three of them sat in silence until Captain Castor asked,

"Well, what do we do now?"

Kate smiled at the captain and placed her hand over his. "We? I think it is Merritt and I who must take it from here, captain. Viola would never forgive us if anything happened to you."

Captain Castor flushed a bright red. "Oh, no, Missy!" he said. "That... that... *barbarian* damaged three of my boats and killed one of my best crewmen. I will play some part in his downfall." Merritt nodded his understanding and signaled the bartender for another round of drinks. After they had raised their glasses in a silent toast, Merritt said, "Then I propose that we go straight at the colonel, drive him and his henchman from Little Torch Key and deliver them directly to the gates of Hell."

Kate stared at Merritt dumbfounded. "You think you can do what the Army could not?" she asked incredulously.

"I do," Merritt answered. "Captain Cox, God rest his soul, was a fool. He broke every tactical tenet I know, from dividing his forces to not dispersing his men while under threat. The rawest shavetail could have handled it better."

Kate leaned back in her chair and crossed her arms. "I knew you to be a stubborn man Merritt, but not a foolish one."

Merritt leaned forward and said, "I have an idea how to deal with Colonel Hollingsworth and what is left of his band of miscreants. Give me a couple of days to work out the details. Will you do that?"

Kate and Captain Castor exchanged glances. "We can do that, Merritt," answered Kate. "But if we find it impractical—or improbable—we will not be able to support you."

The next day, Merritt returned to the pier where they had first landed in Key West. It was bustling with boats loading and unloading their cargos, attesting to the city's growing prosperity after the end of the War. Standing to one side was a small group of men who appeared to be the same ones who had approached Merritt and Kate on their arrival in Key West. When they saw

Merritt approach, they nudged each other and spoke in low whispers.

"Gentlemen," Merritt greeted the men.

One of the men, tall and thin, bald except for a fringe of dark hair, stepped up to Merritt. He swept off his hat and bowed. "Yer excellency," he said. "Do you have more luggage what needs to be carried?" The other men snickered. They were all roughly the same age and were dressed in a mishmash of fashions, from sailors' frocks to various bits and pieces of Confederate Army uniforms. They all felt that Merritt's arrival promised good things to come, either by providing work or presenting some opportunity to cheat or rob him. Either way, a solution where everyone benefits.

Merritt said, "I am Merritt Cowles, and I am looking for former soldiers." The men glanced at each other and then turned to walk away. "I am paying $1 a day for former privates, $2 a day for non-coms," Merritt added.

The thin man turned back and looked at Merritt suspiciously. "Why so much?" he asked. "We sergeants never made no more'n $20 a month. A private? Hell, he got $13 a month, when he got paid at all."

Merritt shrugged his shoulders and said, "I will not lie to you. It is dangerous work I propose."

"Such as?"

"I seek a Union colonel who robbed a payroll and killed my son."

Merritt saw the thin man's eyes light up. Merritt suspected that the man would like nothing more than to have another crack at a Union colonel. The thin man cocked his head at Merritt. "Then what do you say to a bonus of $50 at the end of service, payable to our widows or kin if we do not survive?"

"Agreed," said Merritt.

The thin man held out his hand. "I am Alonzo Stofer, former sergeant in Abell's Light Artillery, 1st Regiment, Florida Infantry Reserves."

"Well, Sergeant Stofer, welcome to the team," said Merritt,

shaking the sergeant's hand. Merritt took the man aside and said: "If possible, I would like you to find ten to 20 men, all combat veterans. I urge you to pick them with care as they may be guarding your back when the firing begins." Merritt pulled out a piece of paper from his pocket and handed it to Sergeant Stofer. "This is the address of a warehouse owned by a friend of mine. Bring whatever men you find there in two-days at 9:00 a.m."

Sergeant Stofer nodded. "Key West is awash in veterans," he said. "Even weeding out the drunks and opium eaters should still net us a dozen or so good men."

Colonel Hollingsworth and Cyril sat in the rockers on the front porch of the colonel's cottage. The sun was setting, and a cool breeze ruffled the palm fronds above their heads. The fallen Union troops had been buried and the fragrance of tropical flowers, rather than the dead, once again perfumed the air. Colonel Hollingsworth took deep breaths and thought, *How I love it here!*

"Do you not think it time for us to leave the island, Colonel?" asked Cyril. "They will be back agin, and no measure of traps and gewgaws will stop them this time."

The colonel smiled. "I will make my stand here, Cyril."

"But, colonel, that do not make no sense! We can get more men and pick a better defensive position..."

Colonel Hollingsworth reached over and patted Cyril's arm. "You are a good soldier, Cyril, mebbe one of the best I ever had. But I will fight them here, alone. Do you understand?"

When Cyril started to protest, the colonel said gently, "That is an order, Cyril. We are the only two left now, and to what purpose if we both perish?" Colonel Hollingsworth got up and went inside, returning quickly with a piece of paper. "The remaining money is in a vault in the new Key West cemetery. Memorize the name I have written on this paper and then destroy the note. Do you understand?"

Cyril glanced at the note. *Aubrey Charbonnet,* it read. Cyril looked back at the colonel, tears filling his eyes. "I obey this order under protest, colonel," he said. It was the closest to insubordination Cyril had ever come.

Two days later, Merritt and Kate met Sergeant Stofer at an empty warehouse owned by Captain Caster. The sergeant had managed to recruit fourteen men, all of whom stood sullenly staring at Merritt and Kate. As before, they were dressed in an assortment of mismatched clothes. But Merritt knew they all shared a bond common to combat veterans everywhere: they had looked death straight in the eyes and had persevered. Most felt that they had little more to fear on this earth.

"Gentlemen," Merritt said, addressing the men. "Over in the corner there are new Spencer carbines for all of you and a thousand rounds of ammunition. For the next several days, Sergeant Stofer will train you on the use of the rifles. When the time comes—probably within the next 3 weeks—Sergeant Stofer will also brief you on our mission and the roles you will play. Meantime, please form a line and I will give you a week's pay in advance."

Sergeant Stofer whispered in Merritt's ear, "I do not know that that is a good idea, Sir. They may simply abscond with the money."

Merritt whispered back: "Better they desert us now, sergeant, then when the bullets start to fly."

CHAPTER 22

Preparations

If your enemy is secure at all points, be prepared for him. If he is in superior strength, evade him. If your opponent is temperamental, seek to irritate him. Pretend to be weak, that he may grow arrogant. If he is taking his ease, give him no rest. If his forces are united, separate them. If sovereign and subject are in accord, put division between them. Attack him where he is unprepared, appear where you are not expected. — Sun Tzu, The Art of War

When another 2 weeks had passed, Merritt was able to walk without a crutch, although he still had a pronounced limp. Nonetheless, he believed himself well enough to settle matters on Little Torch Key. He sent notes asking Captain Castor and Sergeant Stofer to join Kate and him that evening at the Crow's Nest bar. Merritt wanted to brief them on his plan to catch or kill Colonel Hollingsworth and what remained of his henchmen. He glanced at Kate, hoping she would find the plan both 'probable and practical'; he had not before shared it with her.

The four of them sat around a table at the back of the bar. With the money Merritt had advanced him, Sergeant Stofer had gotten a haircut and a professional shave, as well as some new clothes; he was almost unrecognizable from the man Kate and Merritt had first met at the pier.

Before Merritt could begin his explanation, Captain Castor asked, "What makes you think they are still on Little Torch Key, Merritt? Were I them, I would have skedaddled long ago."

"He is still there," answered Merritt, with a certainty that surprised them all.

"But how can you be so sure?" Kate pressed. "Weeks have passed since the Army's ill-fated attack on the island."

"Because, in a way, I know Colonel Hollingsworth, as I served with many men like him in the Mexican War. Colonel Hollingsworth was successful under U.S. Grant because they are like-minded: attack, attack, and never retreat." Merritt took a sip from a glass of whiskey. "He will not run away. He is there waiting for us to try again."

Kate, Captain Castor and Sergeant Stofer glanced uncertainly at each other but said nothing. When there appeared to be no more questions coming, Merritt said, "As I was thinking about this, I remembered the story of Timur's attempt to capture Delhi in 1398..."

"Timur?" interrupted Captain Castor. "Who is Timur?"

"Timur was a direct descendent of Genghis Khan," Merritt explained. "As he tried to capture Delhi, he found himself facing a Sultan who had 120 war elephants. Now, these are fearsome beasts, covered with armor and with poisoned tusks..." Kate watched Merritt tell his story and smiled. In her mind, she could see him sitting in a dormitory at West Point, regaling his fellow students with military tactics about which he had just read. "Timur had only camels which were useful only as pack animals," Merritt continued. "But Timur had the idea to load the camels with as much straw as they could carry, light them on fire and drive them at the elephants.

"Timur's plan worked. The burning camels and their screams of pain so frightened the elephants that they turned and trampled the Sultan's men in their hurry to escape. Timur walked into Delhi largely unopposed."

For a few moments, no one said anything. Then, Sergeant Stofer asked, "You intend to send burning camels after Colonel Hollingsworth?"

Everyone burst into laughter, which caused Sergeant Stofer to blush bright red. Kate came to his rescue: "I would do so to keep from losing a single man more. But I do not believe Merritt meant his story literally." Kate tilted her head. "I mean, where would we get so many camels?" This time the sergeant joined in the laughter.

Merritt unrolled a drawing he had brought with him and spread it on the table. It represented the long, vaguely comma-shaped Little Torch Key. "Is this orientation correct, Captain?" asked Merritt. In the drawing, the little island lay aligned almost exactly north-south.

"It is."

"And what can you tell us about the prevailing winds this time of year?"

Captain Castor shrugged. "The trade winds is always easterly, only the gusts and wind speed vary month-to-month. This time of year, I reckon the wind will blow steady around 9-10 knots but can gust up to twenty. 'Course, that ain't counting any other weather events that might occur."

Merritt took a pencil and drew a series of east-west parallel lines across the island; then he drew arrowheads on the lines pointing West. "The wind," he explained. Then he drew a line across the island about a third of the way down. "And this is the extent of solid land, Captain?"

"It is. The south end of the island is all swamps and marshes, full of snakes, mosquitos, and other bitey bugs." The captain then pointed to the north tip of the little island. "If the colonel is still on Little Torch Key, he will be here."

Merritt nodded his head. "Very well," he said, turning to Sergeant Stofer. "And the men?" he asked. "Are they comfortable with their new weapons?"

"Yessir."

Merritt turned once again to his drawing of Little Torch Key.

"Then this is what I have in mind..."

Colonel Augustine "Gus" Hollingsworth sat on the front porch of his cottage, feet up on the railing. He was in a contemplative, almost introspective, mood. This was unusual for a man who rarely tended to look backwards. But the colonel knew that they would be back again soon—whoever 'they' were. The Army, certainly, but who were the mysterious man and woman? The colonel suspected that they might be detectives hired by the Army to track him down.

Do you have any regrets, old man? he asked himself. *No. Well, mebbe... the Reb prisoner, certainly.* Colonel Hollingsworth thought back to that day. He was standing with two junior officers when he noticed a soldier guarding three Rebel prisoners. The guard appeared half-asleep and had allowed one of the prisoners to move behind him out of his direct line of sight. Colonel Hollingsworth started towards the guard to dress him down when he saw the prisoner move as if to grab the guard's musket. The colonel raised his pistol and fired once, striking the prisoner in the face.

All hell broke out. The soldiers in the camp rushed for their weapons, certain there was a surprise attack underway. Other guards cocked their weapons and pointed them at cowering prisoners.

When order was finally restored, Colonel Hollingsworth explained what had happened and the camp returned to normal. And that would have been the end of it, except that one of the other prisoners in the dead man's group was the son of a former South Carolina senator. He immediately began screaming that the man had been murdered as he had never tried to disarm the guard. Investigators could find no one else who had seen the dead prisoner make an aggressive move and the event became so political that the Army had no choice but to hold a court martial.

Colonel Hollingsworth took in deep breaths of the flower-scented air. The only sounds were palm fronds rustling in the breeze and birds chirping. Since Cyril, Sammy and Bear and the sloop's crew had departed the island, the colonel had been left in complete solitude. It suited his mood. He closed his eyes and let his memories slip the boundaries of time and place:

Gus Hollingsworth, aged 10-years-old, sat at the dinner table waiting for his father to react. Gus' mother had just told him that Gus had been caught cheating on an exam at school. Surprisingly, his father had said nothing, and had done nothing.

Gus' anxiety began to build. He had been beaten before for more minor transgressions. Would his father just suddenly explode, tear the belt from his waist and bend Gus over his knee? Or would he disown Gus, banning him from the family and forbidding him from ever using the Hollingsworth name again? The more time that passed, the more Gus' imagination exaggerated his potential punishments.

Even Gus' mother appeared surprised at his father's seeming indifference; she finally asked, "Are you not going to punish the boy?"

Gus' father looked up from his plate. "You cannot beat honor into someone," he answered. "You either have it or you do not."

Colonel Hollingsworth sighed deeply. He knew that despite whatever honor he had gained through his accomplishments on the battlefield, he would only be remembered for killing an unarmed Reb prisoner. And, of course, the payroll robbery. But he felt no remorse or regret about the robbery; as far as he was concerned, the Army had stolen his career and he had merely sought recompense.

But whatever regrets the colonel did or did not have, he had none about his military service. Colonel Hollingsworth's military pedigree went back centuries, in both America and England. It would have been unusual for any young man in his family to choose a different profession. But, in any case, the military suited him. All of his commanders had recognized his tactical and leadership skills and he rose quickly through the ranks.

One day between campaigns, Colonel Hollingsworth had been alone with General U. S. Grant in his headquarters. Grant sat at his desk, feet up, with a bottle of whiskey in front of him. Grant was as disheveled as always; his boots were dirty, his uniform was thread-bare, and his hair looked as though it had never met a comb. "Gus," Grant said, "you and I are a lot alike." Grant made a dismissive gesture. "Not like the rest of my officers who would prefer to talk the enemy to death." Grant poured himself another drink. He did not offer any to Colonel Hollingsworth who was well-known to be a tee-totaler. "I reckon you and I could end this war tomorrow. Jest the two of us. What do you say we grab a couple 'a muskets, march into Rich-mond and hang old Jeff Davis from the nearest hickory tree?"

Colonel Hollingsworth thought for a moment about climbing his observation platform to keep an eye out for the enemy. But he did not bother. *When they come, they will come at dawn,* he thought. *That is what I would do.* The colonel closed his eyes and drifted off to sleep, lulled by a soft breeze and memories of past glories.

Merritt intended to attack Little Torch Key at dawn, but the water around the keys was too hazardous to navigate at night. Captain Castor had suggested that they sail to Ramrod Key, adjacent to Little Torch, and spend the night. They could then attack in the morning at their convenience.

As planned, Merritt had borrowed three boats from Captain Castor. Two were sloops of around one-hundred feet, while the third was the captain's personal yacht, a two-masted, sailboat closer to forty feet. The captain had offered the yacht because it was fast and had a shallow draft. Merritt had tried to lease the boats, but the captain insisted that they were his contribution; and the captain had also insisted on commanding his yacht. Nothing Merritt or Kate could say would change his mind.

It was around 2:00 p.m. as Merritt oversaw the final loading of the boats. Seven of the new men were placed in one sloop and four the other; three men were assigned to the yacht under the supervision of Sergeant Stofer. Merritt watched as four barrels of kerosene—more than 40 gallons in each—were stowed on the deck of the yacht. A dozen or so torches followed. By 2:30, the three boats had left the pier and sailed past Fort Taylor. This time, there were no salutes from the Fort, which loomed ominously, and silently, on their port side. Soon, they were in open water and turned north.

CHAPTER 23

The 3rd Battle of Little Torch Key Begins

Courage doesn't always roar, sometimes it's the quiet voice at the end of the day whispering 'I will try again tomorrow. —Mary Anne Radmacher

K ate and Merritt rode in the sloop with four hired men and a crew of three. When she boarded, Kate had been surprised to see that John Frost captained the boat. Kate rushed up to him and took his hand. "Mr. Frost!" she exclaimed. "I am surprised and delighted to see you!"

John Frost smiled broadly. "Why, thank you, Missus, but why are you surprised?"

"I did not think Captain Castor would permit you to risk your life again. He made it clear to me that he had big plans in mind for you."

"Aye, the captain was displeased when I volunteered," he admitted. John Frost gingerly touched the still-healing scar on his cheek. "But I owe the colonel and his thugs, and I always repay my debts."

The sail to Ramrod Key had been quite choppy, but Merritt appeared to be getting his sea legs. He held on to his lunch and his dignity throughout the trip. As before, Kate enjoyed the time under sail immensely. At one point, a pod of dolphins played in the bow wake, delighting everyone aboard. John Frost had smiled and declared it to be a good omen.

When they arrived at Ramrod Key, the three boats anchored in shallow water on the lee side of the island. The boats were then lashed together so that it was possible to walk from one to another. They were just far enough offshore so that the mosquitos could not find them.

Kate thought the atmosphere on board almost party-like. Captain Castor allowed the men a ration of rum and a fine dinner was cooked on charcoal grills. There was laughter, songs, and coarse jokes—told in low voices, of course, out of respect for Kate's sensibilities. Kate turned to Merritt and said, "I would have expected a more somber atmosphere." Sergeant Stofer, who was passing by, overheard Kate's comment. "Ain't it the bible that says, 'Let us eat and drink, for tomorrow we die'?" he asked her.

Kate smiled. "I think the verse refers to the hope for resurrection: the whole quote is, 'If the dead are not raised, let us eat and drink, for tomorrow we die.'"

Sergeant Stofer grinned at Kate and shrugged his shoulders. "Makes good sense to me either way."

A bunk in the interior of the sloop had been made available to Kate while the men slept on deck. But there was little ventilation below decks and the temperature was uncomfortably high. Kate brought a blanket and pillow with her and found a place away from the men on deck. The breeze was cool and refreshing and the sky was bright with stars; Kate thought about a similar evening in Dover when Merritt had first kissed her. She longed to lie next to him on deck, to feel his warmth and strength. But even in the middle of the Florida Keys, even on the evening before they all may die, there were still some things a lady simply did not do.

All around her, Kate could hear the men snoring. She watched meteors streak across the sky and listened to the gentle lapping of the waves against the hull of the boat, but she could not fall asleep. She prayed that Colonel Hollingsworth and his men had already fled Little Torch Key. And if they had not, she prayed for God to protect them all. If she had any misgivings about Merritt's plan, it was only because the colonel had proved himself a wily and merciless enemy.

Colonel Hollingsworth awoke just as the sun was beginning to paint the clouds a soft, pastel pink. He went to his wash basin, washed his face, and trimmed his beard. Once he had completed his ablutions, he chose his best clothes to wear. *They are coming today*, he thought. *I can feel it in the air.*

The colonel casually climbed the stairs to his observation platform, his brass telescope in one hand and his rifle in the other. He reached the top just in time to see two boats come over the horizon. When he focused his telescope on them, he could see there were actually 3 boats, one considerably smaller than the other two.

Colonel Hollingsworth felt no real anxiety; rather, he felt the familiar adrenalin rush as he mentally prepared for battle. When the boats were close enough to make out some detail, the colonel was surprised; he had expected the boats to be teeming with soldiers. Instead, he could see no more than two-dozen men altogether, including the crew. *Now, that is not what I was anticipating*, he thought. He had believed the Army would return with overwhelming force.

As the distance slowly closed between the small flotilla and Little Torch Key, Colonel Hollingsworth could make out more detail. He was not terribly surprised when he saw a woman standing on the bow of the lead boat. And it was obvious the men were not soldiers; they were a motley group dressed mostly in rags. But each man carried a carbine so new that the sun reflected off it in blinding flashes. *Mercenaries. Probably all former military.* The colonel put down his telescope and leaned against the railing. *Cyril was right,* he thought. *No 'traps or gewgaws' would stop this group.* "Anyway, this should be interesting," he said aloud.

As planned, the two sloops stopped around a mile off the southern end of Little Torch Key, while the captain's faster yacht sped on ahead up the east coast. His mission was to see if any ships were tied to the little pier at the north end of the island. Captain Castor stayed to the far right of the channel, keeping his boat at the maximum possible distance from the coast, hoping to stay out of reach of any sharpshooters on shore.

The yacht reached the northern edge of the island without incidence. There were no boats at the pier and the whole island gave the impression of being deserted. Captain Castor reversed course and sailed closer to shore, daring anyone to take a shot at them. Sergeant Stofer and his four men, crouching below the gunwale, held their carbines at the ready.

When they were halfway down the coast of the island, a single gunshot rang out. The round fell harmlessly in the water, no closer than twenty yards to the boat. Although there was no one to be seen on the shore, a puff of white gun smoke clearly marked the shooter's position. Sergeant Stofer and his men sent volley after volley of rifle-fire into that spot and the surrounding vegetation.

After a minute or so, Sergeant Stofer ordered a cease fire. When the sound of the last gunshot had rolled away across the water, all became silent. The men in the boat braced for more gunfire, but none came. A short time later, Captain Castor ordered the sails set and they headed towards the south end of the island where the two sloops waited for them.

Colonel Hollingsworth was startled when he heard the first gunshot from the island. *What the hell?* He thought that everyone had left the island days before. A moment later came the crash of return gunfire. A great flock of white birds, startled by the gunfire, rose and swirled like a column of white smoke into the cloudless blue sky.

The colonel watched as the small boat hesitated, and then resumed its trip south. He grabbed his rifle, climbed down from the platform, and went to the spot on the shore where the gunfire had been directed. It was not difficult to find. Bullets had cut many of the trees and bushes down to waist level, clearing an area some ten yards wide.

Colonel Hollingsworth quickly found the shooter. Sammy lay on his back, bleeding from multiple wounds. He turned to the colonel and seemed about to say something when a deep sigh escaped him, and he passed away. Next to him was an old, single-shot musket that looked as though it had not seen use since the Revolutionary War.

Colonel Hollingsworth reached down and touched the boy's face. "My poor, brave boy!" he said. "Why did you not leave as I asked?" He picked the boy up in his arms and carried him back to his cottage. There, he lay him in the colonel's own bed and covered him with a blanket. "I do not believe I will live beyond this day. But I promise you, Sammy, I will make them all pay dearly."

When the three boats were once again together, Captain Castor told Merritt and Kate what had happened. "There was but one shot fired from land," he said, "and none after Sergeant Stofer and his men returned fire."

Merritt nodded. " And the pier," he asked. "Were there any boats?"

Captain Castor shook his head no. "But at least we know they are still here. You were right, Merritt."

Merritt nodded and said grimly, "So let us finish it."

Colonel Hollingsworth had returned to his platform. He

watched the three boats confer and then go their separate ways. One of the sloops turned and headed for the small western channel around the island. It appeared to carry four or 5 men, with the addition of the woman and ship's crew. The second sloop turned northwards in the eastern channel, followed closely by the little yacht. This sloop carried the majority of the mercenaries, maybe six or 7 men plus crew. The yacht had a smaller compliment of men and no more than a two-man crew.

Colonel Hollingsworth was fascinated by the scene unfolding before him. He felt like Robert E. Lee must have felt overlooking the Battle of Fredericksburg: omnipotent and untouchable. *Was it not there,* the colonel wondered, *that Lee gave that wonderful quote: It is well that war is so terrible, otherwise we should grow too fond of it.'?*

The colonel was curious as well. Try as he may, he could not understand the choice of boats or the distribution of the mercenaries within them. But then all became clear when one sloop anchored in the western channel while the yacht began a sweep along the eastern coast of the island. The second sloop, containing the most firepower, stood offshore, apparently providing protection for the yacht.

A chill moved up the Colonel's spine. *They intend to burn me out,* he thought, even as he saw the first torch light, and then another and another. Thick black smoke from the torches trailed behind the yacht.

CHAPTER 24

The Battle Begins

Once more unto the breach, dear friends, once more;
Or close the wall up with our English dead!
In peace there's nothing so becomes a man
As modest stillness and humility:
But when the blast of war blows in our ears,
Then imitate the action of the tiger. —*William Shake-*
speare, Henry V

On board Captain Castor's yacht, the men moved with a practiced precision. One man would dip a torch in a barrel of kerosene and hand it to a second man who would light it; then the second man would hand it to a third who tossed the lighted torch into the vegetation along the shore. Captain Castor kept the yacht as close to shore as he deemed safe, and they progressed at a rapid rate. Within a few minutes, the eastern shore of Little Torch key was on fire from the beginnings of the marsh in the south to the northern limit of the island.

As Merritt had anticipated, the trade winds began to rapidly spread the flames across the island. But what Merritt had not expected was the swirling of the winds where water met land. This phenomenon kept thick clouds of dark smoke over the yacht, blinding the men aboard her. When one of the men threw the last burning torch, he threw it directly against an unseen tree and the torch bounced back onto the yacht. The deck, saturated with spilled kerosene, burst into flame, instantly engulfing the entire boat. Men screamed in fear and pain and threw themselves overboard. Ammunition began to explode from the heat, sending brass cartridges spinning through the air.

Waiting several hundred yards offshore, the sloop could not see what was happening to the yacht because of the smoke, but they could clearly hear the men's screams; it seemed as though they would never stop. "What kind of hell is this?" asked one of the men in the sloop. He dropped to the deck and covered his ears. Other men turned away and cried, begging God to make it stop.

Aboard the sloop in the western channel, they could see thick black smoke begin to rise above the island. They were unaware of the yacht's fate, but the growing fire attested to the success of its mission. All eyes were on the western shore awaiting Colonel Hollingsworth and whatever remained of his thugs to make their appearance while fleeing from the conflagration. But seeing anyone on the shore was quickly becoming difficult; the smoke rose hundreds of feet in the air as the fire spread across the island, appearing as a moving wall. First, Merritt and Kate were assaulted by the smell of burning grass and wood, and then ash began to rain down on their sloop. Next came the ever-thickening smoke with glowing embers that danced across the water in the narrow channel, threatening to set the adjacent key on fire as well as the sloop. The crew rushed about putting out sparks that landed on the superstructure and stowed sails.

Visibility was down to only twenty or 30 feet and falling. Merritt and Kate could hear the roar of the flames as they rushed across Little Torch Key. Merritt yelled, "Keep an eye out, men!" *No one could survive that*, thought Kate. *Either they die in the fire, or they come through us.* She checked the load in her carbine and squinted through the smoke at the western shore.

Colonel Hollingsworth dipped his red bandanna in a bucket of water to wet it and tied it across his mouth and nose. He ran for the western shore of the island which was the only escape left to him; even running as fast as he could, he was barely able to keep ahead of the moving wall of smoke and flames. *They will be waiting there for me*, he thought. *But better to take my chances than be burned alive.*

When he arrived at the shore, the colonel grabbed a piece of driftwood for flotation—he was not a strong swimmer—and entered the water as quietly as he could. He was slightly north of the sloop, the shape of which he could just barely make out through the smoke. He could see no one and heard nothing beyond the roar of the approaching fire. The heat from the hungry flames was becoming unbearable and he felt as though the exposed skin on his face was already blistering.

Colonel Hollingsworth quickly weighed his options: he could try to swim across the channel and hope the smoke would hide him from the sloop; or he could attack. The colonel smiled at himself. There was never really any doubt which path he would choose. Besides, he now had something too valuable to waste: the element of surprise. The colonel stripped down to his pants, checked that his knife was securely in his belt, and pushed off from shore.

The dark water was blood-warm and offered the colonel little respite from the heat of the approaching fire; but the smoke was slightly less dense at the surface of the water which made breathing easier.

What little current there was in the channel was running south, taking the colonel towards the anchored sloop with very little effort on his part. And the channel was so shallow, anyway, that he could touch bottom almost all the way across. The colonel tried not to think about what kinds of things lived in the slimy mud that sucked at his bare toes.

Occasionally, the colonel heard men cough on the sloop, but no conversation. He was reasonably certain that their attention would be on the western shore. Therefore, he approached the sloop from the opposite side and pulled himself up on the rudder. Then, he cautiously raised his head above the level of the gunwale.

As he had anticipated, the mercenaries were all lined up facing Little Torch Key, desperately trying to see through the ever-thickening smoke. Standing beside them was the woman and tall man that the colonel had seen through his telescope during the first incursion against his island. The crew was rushing around, frantically putting out small fires caused by the sparks from the flames on the island.

Colonel Hollingsworth studied the layout of the upper deck of the sloop. It was not overly crowded; there was a large tiller on the afterdeck and a raised hatch cover centered on the forward deck. The rest of the deck was kept clear with all lines and ropes neatly coiled and out of the way. Ever a military man, the colonel admired the orderliness of it all.

The colonel carefully raised himself over the gunwale and crept over to a spot behind the hatch cover, but he suspected with the thickness of the smoke he could have sauntered over with little chance of being seen. He had no real plan. He would just react to whatever opportunities presented themselves to him.

Soon enough, one of the mercenaries walked over to the lee side of the boat to relieve himself. The man's eyes were watering from the smoke, and he made his way primarily by feel. The colonel was kind enough to wait until the man had finished before he placed his hand over the man's mouth and simultaneously slit his throat. He held the man until he stopped moving and then let the body sink to the deck.

The colonel wiped his eyes with his bandana and quickly searched the deck around the man's body looking for his carbine.

But he found nothing; it appeared the man had left his rifle with the other men. The colonel sighed and sat down heavily on the deck. He knew that if he had gotten one of the carbines, and with surprise on his side, he could have easily subdued them all. *But now? What is your fallback plan, colonel?* he asked himself. He crawled back over behind the hatch cover and could just make out the men and woman standing against the gunwale watching the far shore through the smoke. He knew that at any moment someone would come looking for their comrade.

The colonel rose from behind the hatch cover and approached the people standing at the gunwale. Had anyone cared to look over their shoulders, they would have seen him coming. But they did not. The colonel reached up and placed his arm around Merritt's shoulders while he held the blade of his knife against Merritt's throat. "Now step back with me, son," he whispered in Merritt's ear.

Kate saw Merritt's movement out of the corner of her vision. When she turned, she could barely make out Merritt and the man standing behind him from no more than six feet away. When she raised her rifle, the colonel said, "Now, Miss, we can end this now if you want, but I would like to talk first."

"Then lower your knife," Kate answered, "and we can talk." Startled at the sudden appearance of the interloper, the three armed men standing next to her turned and raised their own weapons at the new threat.

"Now boys," said the colonel in a soothing tone, "ain't no reason to get jumpy. This little lady and I are jest gonna have a little conflab and then we can settle this."

"Again, lower your knife, or I will settle this right now," said Kate.

"Then take your shot. But you are as likely to hit your husband as me with all this smoke."

"He is not my husband."

Merritt could sense the colonel smiling. "Not your husband? Now see," the colonel said, "we are talking already!"

"Then have your say, Colonel Hollingsworth. But make it

brief."

"You make my point! You know my name while I know nothing about you or your...partner. Three times you have come to my little island to harass me and now you have reduced it all to ashes. I have to admit to being a little curious as to why."

"I am a Pinkerton detective," Kate said, "and I am here to arrest you for robbery and murder."

"And the gentleman?" the colonel asked.

"You killed my son," Merritt answered.

"Ah, but I have killed so many men. It is the nature of war, you know. Can you not be more specific?"

"He was a guard on the paymaster's wagon train."

"Not the sergeant?" asked the colonel. When Merritt shook his head no, the colonel added, "The sergeant was a brave man. I am afraid I do not remember anything of the others."

The colonel felt Merritt stiffen, and he tightened his grip and pressed harder with the knife. Merritt felt a small rivulet of blood run down his neck. "Easy, son," said the colonel.

"The time for talk is over, colonel," said Kate. "Put down the knife."

Colonel Hollingsworth sighed deeply. "As you wish," he said, and he began to pull the blade across Merritt's neck.

Kate sensed what was about to happen and took her shot, aiming through the smoke at where she believed the colonel's head to be. Someone gave out a cry of pain and both men fell to the deck in a jumble.

Kate stood alone at the gunwale as the sloop made its way back down the narrow channel. She fought back tears, not wanting to appear weak in front of the men; but deep sighs wracked her body and she found it difficult to breathe. When she had regained her composure, she turned and walked over to where Merritt sat in the shade of the hatch cover. He looked pale and the cloth he held at his throat was blood soaked. But he was alive.

Kate sat down beside him, their shoulders and hips touching. "I thought I had lost you," she said.

Merritt reached over and touched her cheek. "It is a good thing you shot when you did. The colonel was in the process of removing my head."

Kate felt no need or desire to maintain propriety as she lay her head against Merritt's chest, her arms around his shoulders. Merritt could feel her trembling. "God surely steadied my aim," she said. "I could see little through the smoke.'

Merritt kissed the top of her head and smiled. "Then I have two things for which to be thankful."

Kate looked up at him curiously and asked, "And what is the other?"

"Why, you of course."

They sat quietly entwined for the twenty minutes it took to rendezvous with the other boats at the south end of Little Torch Key. But their anxiety suddenly grew when they did not see Captain Castor's yacht waiting for them with the other sloop. Even before they had finished tying up alongside the other boat, Kate was frantically asking about the missing captain and his crew.

John Frost, captain of the second sloop, told them about the fire and explosions on the yacht, tears running down his cheeks. But he did not speak of the screams of the dying men; he felt no need to share that part of the nightmare.

CHAPTER 25

The Aftermath

The easiest period in a crisis situation is actually the battle itself. The most difficult is the period of indecision – whether to fight or run away. And the most dangerous period is the aftermath. It is then, with all his resources spent and his guard down, that an individual must watch out for dulled reactions and faulty judgment. –Richard M. Nixon

Merritt sent one of the sloops to search for any survivors—or bodies—along the length of Little Torch Key. Kate and he, along with John Frost and four armed men went directly to the site where the yacht had sunk. Based on what John Frost had told him, he was not optimistic that they would find anyone still alive. But he felt he owed it to Captain Castor and his wife Viola to make every effort to do so.

The site of the sinking was not difficult to locate. Although the yacht had burned down to water level and then sunk, the charred mast still pointed like a finger at the wreck below. It was obvious that no one could have survived on the boat, so Merritt, Kate and several armed men went ashore. But there they found only desolation with nothing but the tallest palm trees unconsumed by the fire. There was no sign of Captain Castor or his crew.

Desolate, the landing party reboarded their boat to wait for the second sloop to finish its search. "How will I ever face Viola?" Kate asked. But before Merritt could respond, John Frost gave out a cry: "There!" he said. "The other sloop is coming around the island."

Kate and Merritt rushed to the gunwale to watch the other boat approach. As soon as the second boat spotted them, her crew fired a red flare into the air. There was a moment of silence and then the crew on Merritt and Kate's boat gave out a cheer and rushed to slap each other on the back. Startled, Kate asked, "What is happening?" John Frost rushed up to her and lifted her off her feet. "It is a distress signal, missus, it means they have wounded aboard." And then Kate and Merritt understood: wounded means there is still life. Tears of joy ran down Kate's cheeks as John Frost whirled her around and around, two dancers to a silent, joyful waltz.

The second sloop approached the first and it was still several feet away when Kate leapt across the water and onto its deck. She rushed to the foredeck where she saw three bodies covered by a single sailcloth tarpaulin and two men sitting against the gunwale. *Five men*, she thought, *out of a compliment of eight.* She stood over the two survivors and did not at first recognize Captain Castor; his eyebrows had been singed off as was most of his hair. The captain had severe burns on his arms and appeared to be in great pain. His eyes were closed, and he moaned softly.

"Oh, captain!" Kate cried.

Captain Castor's eyes fluttered open. "Kate?"

"Yes, captain. It is I and we are taking you home to Viola."

"My crew," he said, tears suddenly springing from his eyes. "I have lost my crew! We must go back and find them," he said, trying to rise.

Kate gently pushed him back down. "Viola is waiting for you." She could think of nothing else to say, either of comfort or false promise. She sat down on the deck next to the captain and held his uninjured hand as the sloops made their way back to Key

West.

As the two sloops sailed past Fort Taylor on their way into the Key West harbor, they fired red flares. Word quickly spread through town that they were returning with wounded aboard, and it did not go unnoticed that Captain Castor's yacht was missing. Even before the first boat had tied to the pier a large crowd had already gathered. Viola Castor stood at the front of the crowd, her arms crossed and a look of resignation on her face.

Kate and Merritt stood on the foredeck scanning the crowd as the boat was secured to the pier. Spotting Viola, Kate waved her arms and yelled, "Viola! Over here!" When she had Viola's attention, she yelled, "He is alive!" On the pier, Viola fell to her knees. "Oh, thank God," she said, over and over again.

The crowd on the pier parted to allow the sloop's crew to unload the dead bodies. Then the burned men were helped ashore where a group of women immediately attended to their wounds. Viola held her husband's hand as his clothes were cut away and an ointment applied to his burns. Clean sheets were found to cover the wounded men and arrangements were made to take them home.

The crowd was mostly quiet except for the cries of women and children who had just learned that their husbands and fathers would not be coming home. But there was a general curiosity about the man who had caused so much death and misery. Someone had turned down the corner of the tarpaulin which covered the dead men to expose Colonel Hollingsworth's face. His expression was so restful that, were it not for the bullet hole in the center of his forehead, he might have been mistaken for being asleep. One of the newly grieving widows had to be restrained from attacking his corpse.

Kate sensed that Merritt was near exhaustion. He stood hollow-eyed and unmoving, wincing at every cry. There was no bravado left in him, no obvious exultation over the death of the man who had killed his son and tears glistened in the corners of his eyes. Kate had never loved him more than she did at that moment.

Cyril Winebrenner was drinking beer in the *Forecastle Pub* on Duval Street when word spread that 'Cowles' Army' was returning to Key West. It was also said that Captain Castor's yacht was not with them and that a distress signal had been fired. Cyril had to smile. He had never believed that the colonel would survive another attack, but neither had he ever doubted that he would exact a dear price.

Cyril placed some coins on the bar and walked to the pier. When he arrived, they were already offloading the dead and wounded. He stood to the side of the crowd as the names of the dead and missing were announced; some women screamed, some fainted and others stood silently clutching small children in obvious shock. For an instant, Cyril almost felt some empathy for them. *But their men chose this fight, did they not?* he asked himself. Then he buried this brief moment of near-compassion with what he felt were other useless emotions—love, kindness and mercy, for example—somewhere near the bottom of his soul.

Cyril joined a line of people walking past the dead men. Only the face of the colonel had been exposed and Cyril half-expected people to spit on it as they passed. But he was surprised when most of them said or did nothing, a few even crossing themselves or saying a brief prayer for the dead as they passed. Cyril stood staring down at Colonel Hollingsworth as long as he dared to without drawing attention to himself. Then he turned away, made his way through the crowd, and returned to the *Forecastle Pub*.

Two weeks later, Captain Castor had recovered enough to receive visitors. Kate and Merritt arrived at his home to find that

Viola had shaved his beard and cut his hair. Although there were still bald spots where tuffs of hair had been burnt away, he was once again at least recognizable. He sat shirtless, his left arm covered in bandages, with a comforter across his lap.

Kate bent down to kiss the captain on the cheek and then sat down opposite him, sharing a sofa with Merritt. Viola hovered nearby, ready to do whatever the captain might need. Kate noticed how much Viola had aged over the past two weeks; the wrinkles around her eyes and mouth had deepened and her hair had gone from grey to white.

"We wanted to tell you how much we appreciate your help in dislodging Colonel Hollingsworth, captain," said Kate. "We know you paid a terrible price."

Captain Castor sighed. "Not I so much as my crews." Then, "Were there no other men with him?"

Merritt shook his head. "There did not appear to be. We subsequently searched Little Torch Key and found no bodies."

"It is always possible they left before the attack or even managed to get past us in the heavy smoke," Kate added. "But whatever is left of the snake, it has no head."

"Aye," said Captain Castor. "The world is a safer place without that evil man."

Cyril walked into the Key West Cemetery and over to the furthest corner which was used to inter paupers and criminals. The graves there were unmarked, but one spot had recently been disturbed and that is where Cyril believed Colonel Hollingsworth to be buried. Cyril knelt and dug a shallow hole with his hands where he placed a $20 gold coin. After refilling the hole, Cyril stood up and said aloud: "Mebbe you can bribe your way out 'a hell, colonel; that is surely the only hope for men like you and me."

CHAPTER 26

Three Weeks Later

The appearance of love seems totally irrational, inexplic-able and without reason. Yet, when it happens it feels like the only thing that makes any sense. True love, I guess, is when it keeps on making sense after you actually get to know the other person. —Charlie Maclean

Merritt lay in bed unable to sleep. What now? he wondered. He had taken retribution upon the men who had murdered his son, but it did not bring his son back to him, and now Merritt could find little purpose to his own life. He got up and went downstairs to the parlor where he poured himself a brandy. He sat in the darkened room, the only sound the tick-tock of the mantle clock and the only light a sliver of moonlight that slipped in between the closed draperies.

Merritt thought back to the day Kate left Key West to return to Chicago. They would have traveled back to the mainland together, but Merritt had to remain in Key West a few days longer; he had various accounts to settle, and Kate was needed at the Agency. As they waited for Kate to board the steamer, they stood side-by-side, Kate's hand resting gently on Merritt's arm. They said little until the gangway was opened and people began to board. Even then, their goodbye kiss was awkward, almost perfunctory. Promises were made to write to each other and then Kate was gone, swept up by the crowd boarding the ship.

Merritt poured himself another drink and sat back down. He wondered why Kate and he had never discussed what they would do when their case was finished. Perhaps they wanted to pretend that their time in Key West together would never end. But each knew that the warm, clear nights and perfumed air of the tropics was transitory, having little to do with either banking or detecting.

The two daguerreotypes on the mantle were mere smudges in the darkness, but Merritt could see the images clearly in his own mind. He stood up and walked over to them. It was the first time since Allen had died that Merritt was able to smile at his son's earnest pose in his new uniform. Merritt did not realize it yet, but he had reached the point in his mourning that there was room for both sad and happy memories. As he continued to heal —after all, mourning is nothing more or less than a healing process—it was to be hoped that the happy memories would at least balance the sadness that would never completely go away.

Merritt went back to bed to try to sleep, but he saw Kate's face every time he closed his eyes. He wondered whether she too sat in the darkness pondering what might have been. Finally, he gave up on sleep and went down to the kitchen to light the stove. When he had boiled some coffee, he took a pen and paper and began to write.

Allan Pinkerton sat at an old banker's desk in a small alcove off the main floor of his Detective Agency. It was his favorite place in the world. He loved the musty old smell of the building and the low buzz of conversation from the floor where the clerks and detectives worked at their desks. It sounded like the purr of a well-oiled piece of machinery, which it was.

Agnus Germain, Pinkerton's secretary for more than a dozen years, walked into the alcove and handed him a pile of telegrams.

"Good morning, Mr. Pinkerton," she said. "I just picked these up from the telegraph office."

"Good morning, Mrs. Germain. And thank you." Pinkerton glanced at the telegrams briefly and was about to add them to a pile on his desk when one name caught his eye: 'Merritt Cowles, Sr.' Curious, Pinkerton read the telegram and then gave out a loud grunt. Mrs. Germain, who was walking out of the office, turned to see what he was laughing at. "Is everything alright, Mr. Pinkerton?" she asked.

"Everything is well, I would say. Very well. Would you please see if Mrs. Warne has arrived yet and ask her to come see me? Tell her it is urgent." When Mrs. Germain left, Pinkerton lit a cigar and leaned back in his chair. He had grown quite fond of Kate over the years she had worked for him. They were closer than simply employer and employee, if not exactly confidants. But he had learned to read her moods, and her mood since she returned from Florida was black. She will speak to him only of the mission and nothing beyond it. But Pinkerton, ever the detective, had his own suspicions of what the real issue is.

When Kate arrived at his office a few minutes later, Pinkerton asked her to sit down. A look of concern crossed Kate's face. "Is everything alright, Mr. Pinkerton? Mrs. Germain told me it is important that you see me."

"Nothing to be concerned about, Kate. I have a new case for you."

Kate looked disappointed. "Ah, about that," she said. "I was hoping to take some time off to visit my mother in New York. Would it be possible to assign this to someone else? At least for a few weeks?"

Pinkerton blew a smoke ring at the ceiling. "I am afraid not. One of our best clients has asked specifically for you. And you know our motto…"

"'We never sleep'"?

"No, the other one: 'always keep the boss happy.'" Pinkerton handed Kate the telegram and added, "He is apparently in a bit of a rush."

◆ ◆ ◆

Merritt was sitting in the lobby of the St. Cloud Hotel in Nashville when a Bellboy tapped him on the shoulder. "For you, Sir," the boy said, handing Merritt a folded piece of blue paper. It said simply, 'I am in the Lobby Bar -Kate Warne.'

Merritt rose from his chair and walked to the entrance of the bar that occupied one corner of the lobby. Inside he saw a woman sitting alone at a table in the back. She was wearing a brown skirt and a yellow jacket closed at the neck. On the chair next to her lay a brown fedora.

As Merritt approached, Kate looked up and gave him a smile so bright it was as if the curtains had suddenly been opened and sunlight flooded the room. "Merritt!" she said, rising from her chair. Merritt said nothing as he took her in his arms and kissed her. Then they stood unmoving, locked in each other's arms, for what seemed like hours. Finally, Kate said, "I fear we are making a spectacle of ourselves." Reluctantly, Merritt let her go and they sat down, side-by-side at the table.

"You know, you cannot just keep hiring me when you want to see me," Kate said, smiling. "My boss will figure it out one of these days."

Merritt smiled back. "I wanted to see you here, at this very spot, and I could wait no longer."

"But why here? Surely, we could have met in Chicago or Columbus, or even Key West."

Merritt blushed and mumbled something incoherent. Kate cocked her head at him, and he tried again. "Because I fell in love you here. Right here."

Kate reached for Merritt's hand. "Here?" she asked. "But we had just met!"

"I was lost the moment you first smiled at me. I knew it even then."

Kate squeezed Merritt's hand and they sat quietly for a few moments. Then he said, "I never again want to feel the loss I felt when you boarded that steamer alone. I was such a fool to let you go."

"But everything comes to an end, Merritt. This trip, the next trip..."

"Not this trip, not the next," Merritt said. "I want to marry you, Kate. I cannot stand the thought of a lifetime of transitory good-byes between us."

Kate sat wide-eyed, staring at Merritt. "Well?" he asked.

Kate's mouth opened but no words came out. "You do love me, do you not?" Merritt pressed.

"Well, yes, of course I do. But my work, I do not know that Mr. Pinkerton can spare me right now..."

"Pinkerton and I have already discussed that. He believes that you have earned some time off, as much as you like."

Kate smiled. "Why that old fox!" she said. "I wondered why he kept grinning at me when he thought I was not looking."

Merritt squeezed Kate's hand. "He is very fond of you. He grilled me very thoroughly about my character and intentions. I was quite exhausted by the time he finished."

Kate touched Merritt's face and said, "Well, it looks like my two favorite men have come to an agreement. How can I differ?"

"Is that a 'yes'?" Merritt asked.

"That is a very big 'yes,' Mr. Cowles."

Kate decided that the wedding would be held in Elmira, New York, close to her elderly mother who lived in a small town called Erin where Kate had been born. Erin itself simply did not have the facilities to host a wedding of any size.

Neither Kate nor Merritt wanted a large wedding, but it seemed impossible to keep the guests below 200 people. Merritt's friends and political contacts clamored for an invitation, while Kate's fame also tended to inflate the numbers. After struggling with the guest list for several days, Merritt threw up his hands and said, "This is ridiculous. I propose that we open the wedding to everyone who cares to attend. The same with the breakfast following the ceremony."

"Everyone?" asked Kate.

"Everyone. The whole town of Erin, the whole City of Elmira!"

Kate laughed. "You are very generous, Mr. Cowles! But how does one invite 'everyone'?"

"Elmira must have a newspaper, do they not?"

"The Elmira Gazette, a daily newspaper," Kate answered.

"Well, there you go!" Merritt held up his hands as if bracketing a newspaper headline. "You are all invited to the wedding of Merritt Cowles, Sr. and Mrs. Kate Warne, late of Chicago and Erin, New York."

"You cannot be serious, Merritt!"

"I am very serious, my love. If I could, I would celebrate with the whole world!"

Kate laughed again. "Then we best look for a larger tent for the celebratory breakfast."

CHAPTER 27

Love and The Presbyterians

I hope you don't mind/I hope you don't mind that I put down in words/How wonderful life is while you're in the world –Elton John, Your Song

Merritt accompanied Kate to visit her mother in Erin, New York. It was early November and the peak season for the fall foliage had already passed, but there was still enough color left in the trees to make Kate's heart soar. Despite all her travels, she still felt a deep affection for her 'home' in the rolling hills of western New York. "Is it not beautiful?" she asked Merritt as the train in which they were riding made its way across the Allegheny Plateau towards Elmira, New York.

"It is," Merritt answered. "Are you excited to see your mother?"

"Oh, yes! It has been too long. I sent her early word of our betrothal, and she is very excited. I fear she has already planned out our entire wedding!"

Merritt laughed and squeezed Kate's hand. "I have little doubt that you can direct things as you wish."

"Oh, my poor Merritt! You have yet to meet my mother. I would rather face three angry Union generals and an armed Confederate brigade than confront her wrath."

When the train reached Elmira, a covered carriage with a

driver and two matched horses was waiting to take them the rest of the way to Erin, some fourteen or 15 miles away. But Merritt dismissed the driver and took the reins himself. Kate sat beside him and covered her lap with a brightly colored blanket that had been provided by the carriage rental company. She was radiant with happiness, and she filled Merritt's heart with joy every time he looked at her.

It took more than three and one-half hours to make the trip to Erin, but the weather was clear and pleasant. And the uninterrupted time gave Kate and Merritt an opportunity to discuss their upcoming life together. Rarely did a moment pass that they were not holding hands or touching at the shoulders.

As they approached the Town of Erin, founded only forty-odd years earlier, Merritt was impressed by the obvious economic growth that had taken place. They passed a sawmill, a grist mill, and a post office, as well as other businesses clearly meant to support the area's farming community. Off Church Street—named for a small presbyterian church built there in 1836—they found the home of Kate's mother. The house was a two-story clapboard building with a porch on the first floor that extended the width of the house. A brick path led from the porch to the edge of the dirt road and the shrubbery beside it were carefully trimmed. Like the town itself, it gave off an aura of newness and well-being.

As if reading Merritt's mind, Kate said, "My Daddy built this house just before he died twelve years ago. He was postmaster and saloon owner for all his adult life. He was a teetotaler himself, but he used to say that rum built the living room, beer the kitchen, whiskey the bedrooms and so on."

Merritt laughed. "My kind of man. Except for the teetotaler part, of course."

As soon as the carriage pulled up to the little brick path, an elderly woman ran from the house and down the path with amazing vigor, shouting, "Katie!"

Kate jumped down from the carriage and ran into her mother's arms. Kate waved at Merritt to come over. "And this is Merritt,

Momma."

Merritt bowed slightly and took the old woman's hand. "It is a pleasure to meet you, Mrs. Mitchell."

Kate's mother smiled and said, "It is my pleasure, Merritt. Now please take the horses around back and settle them in the stable. Katie and I have some catching up to do."

Merritt had to laugh as he untacked the horses and put fresh hay and water in their stalls. He had felt the almost overwhelming urge to salute when he had been directed to care for the horses. *Kate is right*, he thought. *Her mother is clearly a force to be reckoned with.*

When Merritt returned to the house, he followed Kate's and her mother's voices to a small parlor. There they sat laughing and holding hands on a black horsehair sofa facing a small fire in the hearth. Merritt sat down in an armchair cattycorner to them. He had a moment before their attention turned to him and he used it to study his future mother-in-law: she was easily a head shorter than her daughter, but she had the same green eyes, dark brown hair—albeit streaked with grey—and slight build. Her posture was erect, and her voice was firm. Merritt was sure that he heard just the smallest hint of an Irish brogue when she spoke.

When the conversation came around to the wedding, Kate and Merritt expressed their desire to have the wedding within a month. Kate's mother was aghast: "Why, that is impossible!" she said. "You must first meet with one of the pastors to make application to be married as well as to discuss the order of worship and whatever premarital preparation you must complete. Church rules mandate that you must schedule this no less than three-months prior to the ceremony."

Merritt looked at Kate. "Premarital counseling?" he asked.

"Oh, yes," answered Kate's mother. "The Presbyterian Church takes marriage very seriously. After meeting with you both individually, one of our pastors will recommend what course of premarital preparation he feels necessary."

Merritt's face fell. "Oh, it is not so bad, Merritt," said Kate's mother, soothingly. "Most likely he will simply recommend that you meet weekly with him to discuss how to maintain the divine sacrament of marriage in a secular world. And so on."

"There is one more thing," Kate said to her mother. "We will need a larger church than the one here in Erin. We are expecting many guests."

Mrs. Mitchell frowned, then said, "Then I would recommend the Lake Street Presbyterian Church in Elmira. It was built only three years ago, and I have heard that it can serve over 200 congregants."

When Kate and her mother went into the kitchen to prepare dinner, Merritt walked out onto the front porch and lit his pipe. He was lost in thought when Kate walked up beside him and asked, "How are you doing?"

Merritt turned and kissed her forehead. "It is a little over-whelming," he said. "But you are worth it."

"Well, that is good Merritt, because there is one more *tiny* thing..."

"Uh oh. Should I sit down?"

"You cannot stay here before the wedding," Kate said. "I am so sorry, Merritt, but Momma will not have a single man and woman staying together under her roof, even if in separate rooms. I do not think she believes she can keep an eye on us twenty-four hours a day."

"Probably wise on her part," Merritt said as he pulled Kate to him. Her mouth fell open and she blushed. "Why Mr. Cowles," she said. "If you think..."

Merritt laughed. "I will find a boarding house tonight."

Merritt ended up spending the night at the boarding house owned by a church friend of Mrs. Mitchell's. *A suspicious man,* thought Merritt, *might think that the arrangement was premedi-*

tated; I am out of the house but there is still someone to watch over Kate should she wander too closely to my den of iniquity.

Kate and her mother had plans to discuss wedding preparations while they waited for Kate's dress to be delivered from Philadelphia, hopefully within the week. That gave Merritt a free day. He decided to rent a horse and ride from Erin to Elmira.

It was a beautiful autumn day with clear blue skies and a hint of the winter just around the corner; a cool breeze ruffled the fallen leaves and the light had already taken on that cast of winter whiteness. The pace was slow, with neither Merritt nor the horse feeling any need to hurry.

Merritt found the Lake Street Presbyterian Church to be a beautiful white, two-story structure with a red roof and dentil architectural details. The spire was so tall that he had to lean back to see the cross at the top. Merritt found a place to tie his horse and then walked around to the side of the church where he found the offices. He was greeted at the door by the church secretary who took him to the office of Pastor Patrick O'Connor.

"Did we have an appointment, Mr. Cowles?" asked the pastor as he thumbed through his appointment book.

"No, Pastor, but I have ridden over from Erin just to see this beautiful church and speak with you, if I may."

Pastor O'Connor leaned back in his chair. "Of course."

Merritt explained about the upcoming wedding and the need to hold it in Elmira.

"I have heard of none of this. Have you made application for counseling and a wedding service?"

"Not yet. My fiancé is a native of Erin, and we just arrived in the area yesterday. We are hoping to have the ceremony within the month."

The pastor shook his head. "I am sorry, Mr. Cowles, but we require at least three to four months to make all arrangements. I do not believe we could even complete the premarital counseling in four weeks."

Merritt sighed and said, "I understand, pastor. But I thought I would stop by and ask."

Pastor O'Connor stood up and shook Merritt's hand. "I am sure we will ultimately be able to accommodate your needs, Mr. Cowles. But rules are rules."

Merritt was about to turn to leave the office when he stopped and pointed at a small, stained-glass window behind the pastor's desk. An ugly streak of rust ran from one corner and down the wall. "I understand that this church building is less than four years old," Merritt said. "It seems too soon to be having leaks like that."

The pastor sighed and said, "There are some installation problems with the windows. Nearly half of them need to be reseated. But we are not a rich parish, and our budget will not sustain such work."

"Forgive me for saying so, but the leaking windows do detract from the overall appearance. Although my fiancé had her heart set on this church, I am not sure if it will work for us looking like this."

"It saddens me to hear that," said the pastor. He sat quietly as Merritt appeared to wrestle with the conundrum confronting him. Then Merritt said, "But perhaps there is a way..."

After Merritt's return from Elmira, he and Kate sat on her mother's front porch. Kate was incredulous. "You bribed the pastor?"

"'Bribe' is an ugly word, Kate."

"You offered to pay for the window repair if he waived the waiting period for a wedding ceremony. That is a bribe."

Merritt grinned and said, "Do you not prefer November 22 over some nebulous time in March or April?"

Kate pretended indignation and said, "Oh, no you do not! Do not use me as a justification for your corruption of the church at its most basic level!" Then she smiled and whispered, "Of course I do! But for goodness' sake, never let my Momma learn of this."

CHAPTER 28

Wedding Day- November 22, 1865

There's no way to know what makes one thing happen and not another. What leads to what. What destroys what. What causes what to flourish or die or take another course. —Cheryl Strayed

Wednesday, November 22 dawned clear and cool with a heavy frost that quickly melted away as the sun rose. Merritt, Kate, and her mother had spent the night before at a hotel in Elmira in order to make the 10:00 a.m. ceremony. There they saw many old friends and co-workers whom they had invited to the wedding. Kate and her mother went to bed early, but Merritt went to the bar and was the grateful recipient of numerous toasts to his upcoming nuptials.

Kate and Merritt's wedding was the social event of the year in Elmira. "Katie,' as the locals called her, was already famous for her exploits with the Pinkertons; and Merritt was tall, handsome, and rich. Allan Pinkerton attended as did numerous Senators and local politicians. The editor of the Elmira Gazette even sent his wife to gather details of the wedding for the Sunday edition. Every pew was soon filled, and an overflow crowd spilled out into the front yard.

The church had been filled to near bursting with flowers sent to celebrate the happy couple. And the windows, Merritt was pleased to note, were resplendent in the early morning light—with not a rust stain to be seen anywhere.

Merritt and his best man, a cousin of Kate's, stood at the altar. The newspaper editor's wife described the groom's attire as *a frock coat of blue with a flower favor in his lapel. His waistcoat was white, and his trousers of lavender doeskin. The best man wore a frock coat also, but of a more subdued tone.*

But it was Kate whom everyone was waiting to see, and there was a collective gasp as she made her way down the aisle to her husband-to-be. The editor's wife wrote *...rarely have I seen a more beautiful bride! Her choice of dress color was a soft teal and the wedding dress design reflected romance with its subtle softness. The rounded shoulder line and open neckline showcased the bride's graceful neck, while layers of cotton dressed the neck and shoulders as well as the dress' lower skirt. Overall, the dress presented a mystical allure which captivated everyone who saw it.*

It certainly captivated Merritt. He could not take his eyes off Kate as she made her way down the aisle. For a moment, he could not believe that such a wonderful woman was really marrying him. He had to glance around quickly at his best man and the pastor behind him to assure himself of the reality of it all.

The ceremony was brief and to the point. In no more than 20 minutes, Merritt was placing a simple gold band on Kate's finger, and they were pronounced man and wife. At that moment, a huge "Hurrah!" went up from the crowd, so loud that the very rafters were shaken. Now, this was considered quite impolite and was simply not done at the time. The Elmirans blamed it on the less-couth Erinians, but truth be told, many from Elmira had raised their voices as well, so beloved was Katie Warne.

After the ceremony, Mr. and Mrs. Cowles walked straight down the aisle, looking neither right nor left, as was the custom. After a brief stop in the vestry to sign their marriage certificate, Merritt and Kate stepped out the front door of the church where nearly two-hundred people stood waiting to watch them leave for the breakfast. Shoes and rice rained down on them as they ran down the sidewalk to where a carriage waited for them.

Merritt suddenly stopped short, startling Kate. "Is anything wrong, Merritt?" Kate asked.

In his mind's eye, Merritt saw a young man in an army uniform stepped away from the crowd. It took Merritt a moment to recognize him. "Allen!" Merritt exclaimed.

The soldier held out his hand and said, "I have missed you, Daddy."

Merritt sank slowly to the sidewalk. At first the crowd stood in shocked silence until someone shouted, "Blood! He has been shot!" People began to throw themselves to the ground or run away to seek cover. Kate dropped to her knees beside Merritt and took his head in her hands. "Oh, Merritt!" she cried, as a pool of blood began to grow beneath him. "Please do not leave me!" But there was no light in his eyes and his body was limp and Kate knew she had already lost him.

Most people in the crowd had not heard the gunshot or the strange fluttering sound the projectile made as it sought Merritt. But Allan Pinkerton had, and he could just make out a small puff of white smoke hanging in the air above a warehouse some two-hundred yards from where Merritt lay. "There!" he said, pointing at the warehouse. He pulled a pistol from his shoulder holster and ran towards the building. Several other men, although un-armed, ran with him.

After watching Merritt fall, Cyril Winebrenner had quickly wrapped his rifle in a piece of sailcloth and ran out of the back-door of the warehouse. He passed a drunk who stared straight at him. Cyril hesitated for a moment. He knew he should kill the man, who could identify him; but he could hear the crowd at the church yelling and screaming and he knew that someone would come looking for him at any moment. He turned towards Church Street and ran down the block and out of sight, making good speed for a man his size.

When Pinkerton and the two men with him reached the ware-house, a broken door gave them quick access to the four-story building. Pinkerton and the men ran from floor to floor, heedless of any potential danger, but discovered no one. Then they ran out of the back of the warehouse and onto Baldwin Street.

Pinkerton stood gasping for breath. He looked both ways down the street but saw no one. No one, that is, except an indigent man sitting beside some trash cans and sipping from a whiskey bottle. Pinkerton approached the man and asked, "Did you see anyone run out of the warehouse?" But the man just looked through Pinkerton as if he were not there and returned to his bottle.

Pinkerton raised his pistol and placed it against the man's forehead. "One more time. Did you see anyone run out of the warehouse?"

The man raised his hands. "Do not shoot, yer honor. I have seen no one."

Pinkerton cocked his pistol and the man's eyes widened. "A fat man," he said, gesturing down Baldwin Street. "He run that way, towards Church Street."

"Was he carrying a rifle?"

The man turned the whiskey bottle upside down to show that it was empty. "This talkin'," he said, "it gives a man a thirst, you know what I mean?"

Merritt put his pistol back in the holster and pulled some change from his pocket. "Here," he said, handing it to the man. "Now, was he carrying a rifle?"

The man shrugged. "I could not really tell. He had somethin' rolled up in a white cloth. Come to think of it, it were about the right size."

Kate and Allan Pinkerton sat at the table in her mother's kitchen drinking brandy from a bottle Pinkerton had provided. Kate still wore her wedding dress, stained with Merritt's blood. She had refused her mother's entreaties to change it.

Mrs. Mitchell had left the room to allow Kate and Pinkerton to be alone. Kate had been inconsolable since the wedding and Mrs. Mitchell hoped that Pinkerton, her employer and friend, could offer her some solace.

Kate fought to keep her composure. Pinkerton sat watching her, his own heart breaking at her obvious pain. "My dear Kate," he said. "It is my intention to remain here in Erin until all arrangements have been made. Do not hesitate to call on me for anything you may need, anything at all.'

Kate managed a weak smile. "Thank you, Mr. Pinkerton. You are a good friend." She poured herself another brandy. "In point of fact, there is something that could use your immediate attention."

"Anything."

"I have decided that Merritt should be buried alongside his wife and son in Columbus. I had him for such a short while... It just seems more appropriate."

Pinkerton nodded. "Consider it done. I will locate their cemetery and make all of the arrangements."

"And his estate," Kate added. "I want none of it. Please see if you can locate any of his relatives. If not, I will make a gift of it in his name to the Lake Street Presbyterian Church in Elmira. I shall call it," she said, laughing through her tears, "the Merritt Cowles, Sr., Perpetual Stained-Glass Window Repair Fund.'"

Cyril Winebrenner sat in a first-class compartment on a train from Elmira to Buffalo via the small town of Hornell, New York. Other than his wrapped rifle on the seat beside him, Cyril had the compartment to himself. He leaned back in his seat and thought, *I could get used to this.* And why not? He was now a very rich man with all shares of the robbery defaulting to the last survivor. He patted the bank passbook in his pocket. The bank in Key West had assured him that they could wire any of Cyril's funds to any other bank he chose. *The world, as they say, was his oyster.*

Cyril did not think much about his day's work, preferring instead to imagine the life of peace and plenty that awaited him.

Not that he did not have regrets; he did, although none were about the morality of the killing itself. He knew, for one, that he should have killed the homeless man. Cyril had no doubt that the authorities now had a description of him. But he did not believe that would matter for much longer. And second, he wished he could have killed the woman as well. He remembered her as he had seen her through his telescopic sight, beautiful and representing everything he detested; to Cyril, she was the pretty little girl at the playground who made fun of him because he was fat and could not run or climb as fast as the other boys. Had Cyril and she passed on the street, Cyril knew she would look right through him and step around him like dog dung on the sidewalk.

Cyril closed his eyes and tried to fall asleep. He knew that there had not been enough time for a second shot, especially with everyone screaming and running around. But that was little comfort to him. Finally, he fell asleep, lulled by the click-clack of the train wheels and the gentle rocking of the car.

CHAPTER 29

Saskatchewan- One Year Later

I will hurt you for this. I don't know how yet but give me time. A day will come when you think yourself safe and happy, and suddenly your joy will turn to ashes in your mouth, and you'll know the debt is paid. —George R.R. Martin

The Colony of Saskatchewan in Canada was comprised of two distinctly different geographic areas. The southern two-thirds were an extension of the Great Plains of the United States while the upper third was primarily glacial lakes and boreal forest. This resulted in a diversity of both commerce and attitude within the colony. While those who lived in the south reveled in the endless vista, the spectacular sunrises and sunsets and the seemingly infinite sky, those in the north worshiped nature in the most basic sense. They hunted and they fished, and they exulted in the seclusion.

Cyril had bought nearly five-hundred acres of rolling hills, pines, spruces, and larches along Lake Athabasca near the settlement of Fond du Lac in the north. Fond du lac was almost completely isolated during the winter and had a population of no more than fifty, mainly people of Dene and Métis descent. But there was a constant flow of traders through the area for the rest of the year and Cyril could send and receive mail that way. He kept in occasional touch with his bank in Key West, if for no other reason than to keep track of his money.

Although Cyril had little contact with the indigenous people, he was well-known to them. He had been seen killing a deer from more than four-hundred yards away with his long rifle, giving him an almost mythical status as a warrior. And, although it was rare, Cyril was occasionally seen in Fond du lac picking up mail or supplies he could not grow or hunt himself, mainly salt, sugar and coffee. For the most part, Cyril spent his days alone, hunting and fishing. But even Cyril occasionally yearned for human companionship. After one long winter when the daily high temperature never rose above zero, Cyril had gone looking for a wife.

His search turned out to be easier than Cyril had expected. Because of his reputation within the Métis tribes—and perhaps because of an overall shortage of eligible bachelors in northern Saskatchewan—he was presented with several candidates. For the first time in his life, Cyril was not judged by his size, at least not negatively, because the indigenous people widely believed that his portliness suggested wealth and stability. Fathers travelled from miles around to introduce their daughters to him.

One girl immediately caught Cyril's eye. She was a 17-year-old mixed-race Métis girl named Marie Amyot. Her laughter was music to what was left of Cyril's soul, and he often found himself lost in her large, brown eyes.

Marie insisted that Cyril and she be married in a Métis ceremony in front of her family and friends. The date was set for two-months hence, early spring, and before the annual black fly scourge would emerge to torment the guests and wedding party alike.

When the day came, the bride, groom and the wedding party all dressed in traditional Métis attire, from ribbon skirts and voyageur shirts to colorful sashes and vests. Because Cyril had insisted that money was no object, smudgers, fiddlers and singers had been hired to augment the proceedings.

The wedding site was a clearing in the forest decorated according to Métis practice. In front of a ceremonial tipi, there stood an archway made of cedar branches freshly cut from the surrounding woods. And to one side was a fire pit with a huge cast-iron pot in which to boil corn.

Before the ceremony began, the wedding party and guests were smudged with the smoke of sweetgrass, sage and cedar to cleanse their sins and encouraged to take a short walk through the forest. Then they were guided back to the clearing by the sound of the drums, fiddlers and singers and the smell of smoke from the fire.

The wedding was truly a community affair. Marie's grandmother said a prayer for the couple and hunters and fishermen brought vast quantities of meat and fish to feed the guests. Marie also had her 'maidens,' the exact number of which Cyril was never able to ascertain, as they seemed to be in constant movement, giggling and preening for the young men; he himself had several 'warriors' to guide and assist him. The local chief, who conducted the Métis marriage ceremony, wrapped the couple in a blanket while they were being smudged again and whispered to them promises of heaven and years of rainbows and companionship. There was also the local priest, Père Brocher, who was present to insure that all religious interests were adequately represented.

The year following Cyril's wedding was one of the best years of his life. He hunted and fished, and Marie kept him company during the long artic winter nights. Marie was comfortable with long periods of silence, which suited Cyril well. But when the mood struck, she would regale Cyril with fantastical stories she learned as a child about the origin of the earth and its inhabitants. Cyril, in turn, told her about life in the big city, which she found both fascinating and unfathomable.

But for a man like Cyril, contentment was a dangerous thing.

The 'old' Cyril would have heard the soft footsteps outside his window late one May night. But he did not. Neither did he hear the soft whisper of brush being piled against the side of his cabin, or the crackle of the first flames.

Marie sat up straight in bed. "Cyril!" she said, shaking him. "I smell smoke."

Cyril reached for some matches and lit a small lantern next to the bed. But the light invited a barrage of gunfire from somewhere outside. Bullets tore through the window and slammed into the wall between them and around them. Cyril and Marie threw themselves on the floor. Cyril reached up and turned off the lantern just as another volley of shots tore through the window.

Smoke was beginning to fill the cabin. Cyril inched up beside the shattered window and yelled, "Who are you and what do you want?" But he was answered only with silence.

Cyril motioned Marie to come to him, and he whispered, "We must get you out of here."

"But who are these people, Cyril, and why do they wish us harm?"

Cyril placed his hand on her arm. "It does not matter. But I will not have you die because of me."

The smoke was becoming denser by the moment and Cyril could hear the roar of the flames as they began to engulf the cabin. Escape would soon be impossible. He yelled out the window: "I am sending my wife out. Do not shoot her and you will have no difficulty with me."

As before, there was no answer. But there were no gunshots, either. Marie shook her head defiantly, "I will not leave without you." Cyril grabbed her arm and dragged her to the doorway, her cries like a knife to his heart. He opened the door and yelled, "She is coming out! Do not shoot!" Cyril shoved her out into the night and slammed the door behind her.

The seconds seemed as centuries to Cyril as he awaited any

gunshots. But when none came, Cyril once again allowed himself to breathe. He looked around but saw no way to escape. Resigned to his fate, he picked up a pistol and opened the door a crack. "I am coming out!" he yelled. "I am not armed."

Cyril stepped out of the cabin with the pistol held behind his back. He was surprised to see only one figure standing in the shadows. As he stepped closer, he suddenly realized who it was. "You!" he said, whipping out the pistol from behind his back.

Kate walked her horse east on Ackerman Road in Columbus, Ohio and then turned north on Olentangy River Road. It was late May, and the air was already hot and heavy with moisture. There was no breeze and dust swirled around the horse's hooves, hanging in the still air long after the rider had passed. She was wearing a riding habit made of dark black cloth with a loose coat closed at the wrist with a velvet cuff. The rest of her attire included a small linen collar with a necktie, black gloves, and a low-crowned hat with a black veil.

Kate carefully followed the written directions provided by her hotel. She had not been able to bring herself to visit Merritt's grave before. But she had mourned long and deeply for Merritt, and although there would forever be a part of her heart missing, it was time for her to move on. She needed to say good-bye.

It was not difficult to find the Cowles family plot. It was marked by a ten-foot tall granite obelisk dedicated to Merritt's father. Smaller stones marked other family members. Three such graves lay just a little to one side of the obelisk. The stone markers had no dates, only names: Sadie McQueen Cowles, Merritt Cowles, Jr., and Merritt Cowles, Sr.

Kate unwrapped the flowers she had brought with her and divided them between the three graves. But on Merritt's grave, she added a sprig of jasmine. Kate stood quietly while she composed herself, refusing to let her emotions flood over her and drown her. Then she reached into her pocket and pulled out the hexagonal bullet on a rawhide lace that Cyril had worn around his neck and placed it on Merritt's grave. "It is over, my love," she said. "Sleep well."

THE END

AFTERWORD

One of the challenges of writing historical fiction is to meld the history and the fiction to the degree possible: i.e., the history must be accurate, and the fictional actions of any real-life characters must be plausible. One would not expect, for example, Abe Lincoln in a fictional setting to be buying and selling slaves. I can see the reviews now: 'If the author had bothered to do any research at all, he would have known that Lincoln was a staunch abolitionist...' But more importantly, the reader would have lost trust in the writer and, probably, interest in the story.

So why use real historical figures at all? Well, some, like Kate Warne, just seem to exemplify certain eras. In my mind, Mrs. Warne personified the new, post-Civil War female, strong, independent, and brave. She entered a man's world and became one of the best of the best detectives of her time, famous for saving Lincoln from assassination in Baltimore and for recovering tens of thousands of dollars in embezzled and stolen money. But to keep true to Mrs. Warne's actual character is difficult, as little is really known about her prior to her employment by Allan Pinkerton. This piece from Wikipedia sums it up pretty well:

> "Very little is known about Kate Warne... except that she was born in Erin, Chemung County, New York and was a widow by age 23. Pinkerton, in his book The Spy of the Rebellion (1883), described her as: [a] commanding person, with clear cut, expressive features ... a slender, brown-haired woman, graceful in her movements and self-possessed. Her features, although not what could be called handsome [beautiful], were decidedly of an intellectual

cast ... her face was honest, which would cause one in distress instinctly [sic] to select her as a confidante."

I wanted to know Mrs. Warne better. I believed that the more I knew about her, the more fairly I could treat her in my novel. But although I consider myself a fair researcher, I could learn little beyond her Wikipedia biography. So, I turned to my friend Dr. Charles J. (Skip) Reilly, an accomplished genealogist. "Skipper," I said, "I have a challenge for you." Little did he know what he was getting into, genealogically speaking that is.

The weeks passed as I waited anxiously to see what he would uncover. When his report finally arrived, the first two sentences read, "Kate Warne is an enigma... The short of it is that her family origin and background is unknown and subject to speculation." I was shocked. The most famous female detective in the world, the savior of Lincoln, how could that be?

Dr. Reilly, a true academic, took five pages to explain why he could find nothing new about Mrs. Warne. His explanation was compelling and revealing at the same time. After all, the 19th century was a world apart when it came to women's rights and societal expectations for their behavior. Dr. Reilly noted what is rumor, what is conjecture and what he could verify:

- She was born in Chemung County, New York, possibly the town of Erin. Dr. Reilly **could not verify** this. He found no birth records and no obituary.

- Her age at the time she began her employment with Pinkerton was 23 years. **Could not verify.** Again, no birth record and no obituary. And, interestingly, her tombstone gives her date of death but no date of birth.

- Her parents were Isarel [sic] Warne (aka Warn, Wain, Warner and Worn) and Elizabeth Hurlburt-Warne. **Could not verify.**

- Her given name was Kate Warne. **Could not ver-**

ify. Pinkerton himself gives a list of aliases Mrs. Warne used, including Kay Warne, Kay Waren, Kay Warren, Kate Warne, Kate Waren, Kate Warren, Kitty Warne, Kitty Waren, Kitty Warren, Kittie Waren, Kittie Warne, and Kittie Warren.

- Kate Warne is the 'Kate Warn' in the 1860 U.S. Census living in Nelson, Illinois. **Could not verify.** The age does not match, and Mrs. Warne was working in Chicago in 1860 and was not likely commuting from Nelson over 100 miles away.

- We know what she looked like. There are only two known pictures which purport to be Mrs. Warne. **Neither can be verified** as being of her. We have only Pinkerton's description to go by.

- She was romantically involved with Allan Pinkerton. **Could not verify.** They spent a lot of clandestine time together which led to wide-spread speculation about an affair. But Pinkerton himself denied it was so and there is no proof otherwise.

So many important questions remain. Was she ever really married (and widowed)? What tragedies shaped her life? What were her ambitions, her dreams, her failures (we know of her successes)? All these things would help us to know her better and help me to portray her more accurately.

Most of the mystery about Mrs. Warne probably results from the culture of the time; women not married by their early twenties were considered spinsters, so it would not be unusual for a woman to lie about her age and/or claim a dead husband and the title 'Mrs.' On the other hand, if she had been divorced, there was only one basis in those days, adultery. And adultery carried a terrible stigma for both the adulterer and the innocent spouse. Another possible reason for duplicity.

In the end, I learned little new about Mrs. Warne. But I have always felt I had an instinctual understanding of her. I cannot tell you why, and there is no doubt that these feelings colored my interpretation of how she would act in the fictitious circumstances in which I put her. Perhaps, even so many years after her death, I too fell prey to her charms. To paraphrase Teddy in my novel, *The Life and Redemption of Teddy Miller*, "every man who met Kate loved her, at least a little bit."

Made in the USA
Middletown, DE
16 July 2023

35303254R00106